Bolan sighted [the tent] with his grenade launcher.

A camouflage tent erupted, the nylon a flaming blossom that disgorged smoke. Bolan slipped on a pair of goggles to protect his vision, pulling a scarf up over his nose and mouth to filter out the choking cloud created by his incendiary round.

With an inferno suddenly ablaze in their midst, the militia gunmen were distracted. Billowing clouds spread through the gap created by Spelling earlier, pouring out over the pair.

"Move in," Bolan ordered.

Spelling and Bolan charged into the churning cloud, slipping among the militia members. They had finally breached the compound, but the militia was on one side and the commandos were at their back.

The Executioner didn't mind. He'd engineered the crossfire between the two groups. The chaos and confusion were his protective cloak, enabling him to continue his mission of cleansing fire.

MACK BOLAN ®
The Executioner

The Executioner®
Don Pendleton's
PATRIOT ACTS

A GOLD EAGLE BOOK FROM
W🌐RLDWIDE®

TORONTO • NEW YORK • LONDON
AMSTERDAM • PARIS • SYDNEY • HAMBURG
STOCKHOLM • ATHENS • TOKYO • MILAN
MADRID • WARSAW • BUDAPEST • AUCKLAND

Recycling programs
for this product may
not exist in your area.

First edition January 2009

ISBN-13: 978-0-373-64362-2
ISBN-10:   0-373-64362-4

Special thanks and acknowledgment to
Doug Wojtowicz for his contribution to this work.

PATRIOT ACTS

Printed in U.S.A.

Let us take a patriot, where we can meet him; and, that we may not flatter ourselves by false appearances, distinguish those marks which are certain, from those which may deceive; for a man may have the external appearance of a patriot, without the constituent qualities; as false coins have often lustre, though they want weight.

— Samuel Johnson 1709–1784

I've seen too many men who have wrapped themselves in the cloak of false patriotism to excuse their bloodlust and greed. I will not shirk my duty to bring my full weight to bear upon them.

— Mack Bolan

THE
MACK BOLAN
LEGEND

Nothing less than a war could have fashioned the destiny of the man called Mack Bolan. Bolan earned the Executioner title in the jungle hell of Vietnam.

But this soldier also wore another name—Sergeant Mercy. He was so tagged because of the compassion he showed to wounded comrades-in-arms and Vietnamese civilians.

Mack Bolan's second tour of duty ended prematurely when he was given emergency leave to return home and bury his family, victims of the Mob. Then he declared a one-man war against the Mafia.

He confronted the Families head-on from coast to coast, and soon a hope of victory began to appear. But Bolan had broken society's every rule. That same society started gunning for this elusive warrior—to no avail.

So Bolan was offered amnesty to work within the system against terrorism. This time, as an employee of Uncle Sam, Bolan became Colonel John Phoenix. With a command center at Stony Man Farm in Virginia, he and his new allies—Able Team and Phoenix Force—waged relentless war on a new adversary: the KGB.

But when his one true love, April Rose, died at the hands of the Soviet terror machine, Bolan severed all ties with Establishment authority.

Now, after a lengthy lone-wolf struggle and much soul-searching, the Executioner has agreed to enter an "arm's-length" alliance with his government once more, reserving the right to pursue personal missions in his Everlasting War.

Prologue

The man in black threaded the sound suppressor onto the end of his Beretta, set the safety and holstered the gun before turning his attention to the key weapon for this mission. The Beretta M-59 rifle was a paratrooper model, with a metal folding stock. Capable of precision accurate single-shot or devastating full-auto fire, its 7.62 mm rounds could slice through a human body with ease. There was a round in the chamber and the magazine was full.

He was here, in the heart of enemy territory to take out Mahmoud Amanijad. The Muslim firebrand was a vocal opponent of the United States government's procedures in dealing with the terrorist threat that the man had sworn his life to oppose. Amanijad, speaking before the packed audience of fellow fanatics, had been behind a plot to unleash a wave of unholy destruction through the U.S.

The crusader pushed off the safety on the Beretta rifle, setting the selector to single shot, lining up on the target's forehead.

Deep in enemy territory, surrounded by jack-booted, heavily armed thugs in the service of the radical, reactionary government, the lone warrior would need every ounce of firepower to escape the scene unscathed, but not before he sent a message to the enemies of freedom and justice everywhere.

The crowd was on its feet, cheering and applauding the divisive Amanijad, its combined voice and racket shaking the auditorium like an artillery barrage.

The dark-clad sharpshooter partly let out his breath, holding in half as he steadied the crosshairs on the center of Amanijad's black-bearded face.

"Too long has America lashed out blindly for the sake of the nebulous concept of national security," Amanijad began his speech, the crowd's tumultuous response to his arrival on stage fading quickly so that his words could be heard. "In their insane efforts to protect the needs of their money-grubbing backers, they rob the people of their rights and their voice. We are here now to show them that we will not be silenced!"

It was a planned break in the speech. The crowd, as if on cue, exploded into a cacophony of cheers. It was exactly what the sharpshooter had been waiting for. The roar of the crowd at its crescendo would drown out the muffled crack of his rifle. The marksman milked the trigger of the scoped Beretta and a single 7.62 mm round shot out of the barrel, screaming across the auditorium from the catwalk to the stage.

The speaker seized up, his handsome, bearded face replaced by horrific gore. Amanijad slumped to the polished hardwood floor in a puddle of blood.

The sharpshooter watched uniformed thugs race onto the stage. One of them spotted the sniper and pulled his sidearm from a holster.

The crowd exploded in wild panic.

The Beretta, switched to full-auto, snarled, and a salvo of rifle slugs stitched through the bodyguard's rib cage, throwing him across the speaker's corpse. Other security guards spotted the flaring muzzle-flash of the full-auto rifle, and their hands dropped to their guns. The marksman shifted his aim, tapping off a short burst that ripped the head off a second auditorium gunman. He whirled and raced several feet, pistol-caliber bullets ringing and clanging on the metal railing and grating at his feet.

The rifleman paused and spun, firing back at the stage, short precision bursts raking two more uniformed shooters. The sniper turned and raced away.

He sped down the catwalk and kicked open an access door to the roof.

The blaze of the sun lanced down on him, and he felt as if he'd dived through the jet of a flamethrower, but he didn't allow himself a moment's respite. The uniformed shock troopers would call in helicopters and backup vehicles to contain him. One did not blow the head off one of the radical government's beloved own without incurring the wrath of a highly motivated police force.

He closed the folding stock on the rifle and slid down a roof access ladder. It was sixty feet to the ground, and the descent, sliding on the rails, would take several seconds. Gravity pulled him as he glanced around, the battle computer in his mind counting down doomsday numbers as he anticipated the arrival of armed guards.

He reached the ground after ten seconds that felt like an eternity, landed in a crouch and pulled the pistol from its holster. A quick dash through the shadows behind the auditorium would bring him closer to his wheels and escape. His deeply tanned features and a pair of sunglasses would mark him as just another driver in this land.

He charged full-out, racing toward the vehicle. Normally on an operation like this, the marksman would have his pilot, a good man who had been working alongside him for years, sitting behind the wheel. Unfortunately, the wingman was otherwise occupied. The crusader was on his own, and that was okay. Cameron Richards had fought alone before, and he was good at it.

As he closed on his car, another vehicle pulled in front of him. A pair of terrified eyes locked on him, catching full sight of him before he'd pulled on his glasses to disguise his features. There was a brief moment of uncomfortable uncertainty, the vehicle's engine rumbling.

Richards aimed at the driver, a woman whose brown eyes widened at the arrival of the gun-toting commando. She'd seen him, could identify him, could link him to the assassination and possibly to the U.S. government, making a messy political disaster. He pulled the trigger on the Beretta and punched a 9 mm bullet through the open window and into her face.

Richards vaulted across the hood of the dead woman's car and raced to his getaway car. He climbed behind the wheel and fired up the engine.

Tires screeched as he tromped the gas, darting out of the alley and toward a main street. Even as he crossed two lanes, he spotted the shock troopers hot on his heels. Richards hefted the Beretta 59 and leveled it as an LAPD squad car wheeled toward his rear bumper. With a pull of the trigger, the window disappeared in a spray of glass. High-powered rounds tore through the policemen's Kevlar vests, killing the driver and rendering the cop riding shotgun close enough to dead that he didn't feel the impact as his out of control car slammed a parked van.

Richards grimaced, but he had anticipated such a response to his escape route. One police car down and his own wheels had lost their anonymity with the shattered rear window. He ran his car up onto the curb. Civilians scattered in panic. He burst out of the driver's seat, leaving his Berettas behind and charging down into the subway. He discarded the cotter pin he'd yanked from the grenade he'd stuffed under his car's seat.

At the top of the steps, the detonating automobile sprayed violence and horror into downtown Los Angeles. No one would be able to cut through the carnage left at the subway entrance.

The explosion also parted the crowd ahead of him. He had free sailing down to the platform and he vaulted the turnstiles. With the apocalypse detonating above him, the ticket agents weren't interested in harassing him for his fare. Richards raced to the edge of the platform and jumped off, racing into the tunnels.

He'd stored a cache of clothes. It would take only thirty minutes to reach it and fade into the crowd.

One more enemy of the United States was dead, and the message was sent.

Mack Bolan looked over the reports Hal Brognola had assembled. The Executioner had been wrapping up business in San Francisco when Los Angeles became ground zero of an assault.

Bolan paused, looking at the photograph of the automobile where Rosa Trujillo had been murdered. The crime scene photos had been taken before the coroner had removed the body, and Bolan felt a knot of disgust form in his gut.

"Amanijad was a lawyer for the ACLU. He'd just achieved a court hearing for two Arab-Americans who were being held without charges," Brognola explained.

Bolan glanced over to the lawyer's photographs spread on the conference table. His frown deepened as he saw a photograph of a slain police officer, also murdered by the mystery assassin.

"He was sending a message," Bolan stated.

"About what?" Brognola grumbled.

"This speech was in direct response to finally letting two men have their day in court," Bolan said. "Someone didn't want the particulars of that case heard."

"I looked at the files on those arrests," Brognola said. "It was sloppy, speculative work all around. Circumstantial evidence at best."

Bolan nodded. "I heard about the case too. Three

years without seeing a lawyer or even knowing what they were being charged with. They even spent some time in Camp X-Ray."

"Interrogation results were inconclusive," Brognola said.

Bolan picked up the photo detailing the carnage caused by the grenade in the assassin's car. The shootings were acts of efficiency. Minimum firepower for maximum effect. The grenade itself provided a barrier of fire and catastrophe between police pursuit and the escaping killer. The cops would pause to help the dying and wounded, and be slowed with the hunk of burning metal barring the subway entrance.

It was a coldly efficient means of stopping the law.

He stacked the photos and inserted them back into the file folder. The images and information within were burned into his memory. He fought down his anger, cramming it into his reserves of strength to keep his mind clear and analytical. When the time came, the Executioner would take the death dealer down.

CARLO ADMUSSEN LIT UP a cigarette and caught a fierce glare from his partner, Maurice Einhard.

"Do you fucking see everything around you?" Einhard asked.

Admussen glanced around at the crates of rifles and grenades stacked around their warehouse. "Yup."

"So the problem with starting a fire in the midst of all this fucking firepower doesn't ring a bell?" Einhard snapped.

Admussen sighed. They'd had this argument hundreds of times. He wondered if they were becoming more like an old married couple than highly-respected black market arms dealers. "One spark in the wrong spot, and we'll be blown clean to San Francisco," he muttered.

"Don't take that tone of voice with me, Carlo," Einhard grumbled.

"They're securely boxed, the roof has vents, and I'm here at the fucking desk, not out in the middle of our ammunition stockpiles. Rifles aren't flammable and matches can't set off a grenade," Admussen retorted.

Einhard raised his hands in frustration and walked away.

Admussen tapped out some ashes and smirked.

From the shadows, Mack Bolan watched the two men bicker. When Einhard stormed away, leaving Admussen alone for a moment, he stepped from the shadows and wrapped a brawny forearm under Admussen's chin. The limb cut off the man's air and stopped the sudden cry of alarm in his throat.

"Hello, Carlo. You and I need to have words," Bolan whispered.

Admussen croaked softly.

"Don't make a sound," Bolan warned him. He let the dealer feel the hard muzzle of his Desert Eagle against his kidney. "A hole through there will mean a slow, painful death."

Bolan loosened his grasp on Admussen's throat, and the death merchant took a deep breath. He glanced back, seeing the Executioner looming above him, features smeared with midnight black grease paint. Cold, deadly eyes stared out of the blacked-out face, pinning Admussen in his seat with the force of their intimidation.

"What do you need?" the gun dealer asked.

Bolan reached to Admussen's right-hand drawer, pulling out a Glock. He stuffed it under his web belt, out of the black marketeer's grasp. "Information."

"I guess I can't play dumb about why," Admussen said.

Bolan shook his head. "Who bought the Berettas?"

"The guy didn't have a name, unless you count Ben Franklin," Admussen replied.

Bolan's eyes narrowed. "Description."

"Six feet. Brown hair. Brown eyes. Nondescript," Admussen said.

Bolan frowned. "Got the money?"

Admussen looked at the wall next to Bolan. The Executioner saw the wall safe and gestured for the arms dealer to open it.

"We haven't had a chance to get it laundered," Admussen admitted. "Then the shooting happened, and I knew we'd be feeling heat. I didn't realize that we'd be experiencing a visit from the boogey man. I was expecting ATF."

Bolan looked out to the warehouse. Einhard was busy directing his men to pile crates into the trailers of eighteen-wheelers. "Hence the house cleaning?"

Admussen nodded. The safe door clicked, and Bolan leveled the Desert Eagle at the gun dealer's stomach.

"Just in case you have another Glock in the safe," Bolan warned. He opened the safe door, and sure enough, there was a handgun set next to the stacks of bills. It wasn't a Glock, however. Bolan took the Colt Python and put it next to the Glock in his waistband. "Which is the stack of cash the buyer gave you?"

Admussen handed over a wrapped band. "I take it you're not going to give me a receipt for that?"

Bolan glared and Admussen took a step back.

"Ten thousand dollars isn't going to be much compensation for the lives lost because you supplied a psychopath," Bolan stated. "Nor is it going to do much for the families now suffering thanks to your greed."

Bolan put the cash in a plastic bag. Admussen realized

that the Executioner was wearing surgical gloves. "All this money is good for is finding the madman. Prints, serial numbers. Trace evidence. I'll find something."

"And for that, you'll leave me alone?" Admussen asked. Bolan nodded.

"And I forget that I ever saw you," Admussen added.

Bolan shook his head. "The next time you think about selling so much as· a toothpick to terrorists, you remember me."

Admussen's lips tightened.

"Go out and help your buddy. Just don't take your cigarette. I don't want you blowing yourself up before you give me the pleasure," the Executioner warned. "I'll let myself out."

Admussen walked through his office door. He reached the top of the stairs that led into the warehouse and looked back, but the big man had already melted into the shadows, gone from sight.

CAMERON RICHARDS got off the plane in Phoenix, Arizona, and his partner, Willem Noth, met him at the airport.

"What the fuck, Will?" Richards grunted as they met. Noth handed over a small nylon gym bag, containing Richards's favorite pistol.

"Care to be more specific?" Noth asked.

"I thought we had presidential sanction in L.A.," Richards grumbled.

"Plausible deniability," Noth explained. "You can't have the White House dancing a jig because we knocked out some Arab mouthpiece."

Richards's eyes narrowed. "So they have a manhunt going for me. I'm fucked."

"Cam, you're swearing again. Have you taken your medication?" Noth asked.

Richards eyed Noth, then grimaced. "Oh, sure. I feel betrayed, and the sudden reaction is 'are you off your meds?'"

"You're supposed to be taking your pills," Noth told him. "You are an operative of the Rose Initiative. You have an image to uphold."

"Image? As what? Some kind of vigilante loose cannon who isn't worthy of praise?"

"Are you off your meds?" Noth inquired.

Richards closed his eyes and took a deep breath. "No."

Noth looked at him closely. "Do you have your bottle?"

Richards fished in his pocket and took out an unmarked pill bottle. Noth pulled out his PDA and checked the contents against the readout he glimpsed.

"It's almost time for your next dose. Humor me and take it five minutes early," Noth said.

Richards opened the bottle and shook out two tablets. "Want one?"

"Fuck you and eat your damn pills," Noth growled.

Richards tossed them into his mouth and swallowed. He opened his mouth and let Noth examine his cheek pouches and under his tongue for unswallowed tablets. "Happy? Let's go get a Coke so I can wash the taste of these out."

Noth nodded, pocketing his PDA. He took a deep breath, then raised an eyebrow.

The pair made their way to the food court, where Richards got a soft drink and an order of fries while Noth sat. The Rose Initiative operative pinched his nose as if searching thoughts trying to escape his nasal cavities.

"What's on your mind?" Richards asked, sucking on his soda through a straw.

"Just thinking," Noth said.

"I'm not going to be given up, am I?" Richards asked, popping a fry into his mouth. "The media's howling for my head."

"We've already got a half-dozen patsies in place, depending on where the investigation takes the government," Noth explained. "All you have to do is lay low until we find you a new assignment."

Richards looked at Noth, his mood darkening as he regarded the liar sitting across from him. "I know too much, despite being an overly medicated little minion," he said.

"The smell from the pill bottle wasn't right," Noth admitted. "Don't make a scene. I have a gun leveled at your gut under the table."

"The Rose Initiative takes out a piece of trash, before it can be revealed that he's their garbage, right?" Richards asked.

"What'd you do? Mold sugar pills to resemble the right medication?" Noth asked.

Richards nodded. "Not that it matters now. You've got the drop on me."

Richards placed a fry between his lips, letting it dangle like a cigarette.

"Spit that out," Noth ordered.

"Oh, come on, let the condemned have his last smoke," Richards replied.

"Spit it out," Noth growled.

Richards spat the fry with blow-gun force, zapping Noth in his left eye. The man's reflexive jerk caused him to pull the trigger, but it also yanked his aim off target. The bullet seared into the lower spine of an elderly man sitting at the next table. The gunshot and the cry of agony created an uproar in the food court, giving Richards a chance to lunge across the table.

Noth realized he'd left himself wide open, despite the gun in his hand. He pulled the trigger again, but Richards had cleared the top of the table, thumbs rammed into Noth's larynx, fingers closing on the back of his neck. The third shot plowed into the tiled floor, panic lashing out like a writhing mass of hungry crocodiles through the crowd. Footsteps thundered, screams mounting, drowning out the third gunshot. Richards wrenched with all of his might, Noth's vertebrae shattering under the force of his powerful hands.

The gun clattered from dead fingers, and Richards charged through the crowd.

He had to contact his pilot, Costell, and get to the base he'd set up for himself. The Rose Initiative would be hot on his heels, and there was no telling what would happen next. Richards let himself be swept along by the running crowds, got out of the terminal and hailed a taxi.

He didn't know why the Rose Initiative had been feeding him behavior modification drugs for the past fifteen years, but suddenly his assessment of the organization's sanction left him alone and chilled. Richards had broken loose from their control, and that made him dangerous. The battles he'd waged across the turn of the millennium to protect his government from deadly threats had been real enough. The Initiative had a stockpile of megaweaponry housed in its Washington, D.C., headquarters, enough matériel to render the surface of the planet uninhabitable for centuries.

Richards stuffed himself and his gym bag into the back seat of the cab.

"Where to?" the swarthy man behind the wheel asked.

Richards rattled off the name of a hotel he frequented while in town. He wouldn't stay in the place, since the Initiative knew he'd go there, but he'd be able to find a dozen places to hole up from there. The cabbie nodded and steered out into traffic, cursing other drivers in his foreign tongue.

No wonder the President had swiftly condemned his actions in Los Angeles, Richards realized. The Rose Initiative had been using him as a puppet. A weapon to keep the public in the dark about the countless threats that were really endangering them. Richards's covert wars kept American citizens from realizing the threats of Islamic operatives and foreign influences on U.S. soil. Rather than smear the menace across the headlines and news programs, they were quietly dealt with so that those who would profit from association with the devils could continue their underhanded deals.

It was all so clear now.

For decades, he'd been a dealer in death, and now, he knew that there was no way to take back the battles he'd waged that had enabled faceless government officials in power. Their chains hung around the American citizenry.

There had to be a way to break that relentless choke hold.

Richards knew of several militia groups who would throw in with him, powerful and trained allies who could help strike several small blows against the dictatorship he'd supported while drugged. Costell would also be a great ally, not to mention Colonel Weist and his mercenary forces.

Still, even with all that manpower, there was no way that Richards could strike a significant blow. The Rose Initiative was a monolithic force.

It would take a blow unlike anything that had been struck before.

Richards thought about the Initiative's deadly stockpile

of weapons of mass destruction. From horrendous, but specific plagues to ultra-low frequency transmitters that could instill murderous rage into entire city populations, they were tools which could carve a new future.

All Richards had to do was break into the stockpile.

That meant distractions, and high-tech equipment.

And an assault on Washington, D.C., itself.

The death dealer nodded, realizing that it would be a suicidal ploy to free the world from its hidden masters, but it would be worthwhile.

Richards realized he had to atone for his wrongs against America.

2

JoAnn Wolfe looked up from the microscope as she examined a sample from the stack of bills. The Los Angeles Crime Lab night shift was no less busy than any other time of the day, but Wolfe had been given a pass on new cases and assigned to examine the evidence sample brought in by Matt Cooper on behalf of the Justice Department.

Wolfe's dark, red tinted hair was tied back and her smooth brow furrowed with a tiny cleft of a wrinkle between her eyes.

"What?" the Executioner asked.

"I've got fingerprints from two sources. Both are in our database. Einhard and Admussen. They're arms dealers. Heard of them?" Wolfe asked.

Bolan nodded. "No fingerprints from anyone else?"

"Not even on the wrapper for the stack. Normally you get impressions, and while I have fingertip shapes, there are no whorls," Wolfe said. "Unless this guy regularly trims his fingerprints, he should have left something, but I've got nothing."

Bolan frowned. "Regular use of solvents would smooth out the ridges."

Wolfe let him look through the microscope. There were round, featureless pads left by skin-based oils on the bill that hadn't developed fingerprint patterns.

"What about the results on the serial numbers?" Bolan asked.

"That's something else," Wolfe replied. "They're discontinued currency, bills originally scheduled for incineration because they were old and tattered."

Bolan looked at the pristine, nearly perfect bill. "Old and tattered?"

"That's according to treasury records," Wolfe stated. "Of course, the look of this money doesn't match the records. Granted, the date range on the bills are correct, but they're so clean they could have been printed yesterday."

"Maybe they were," Bolan said.

"If they were counterfeit, they'd have to have access to the right paper and ink stocks, and the plate patterns are perfect," Wolfe stated.

Bolan nodded. "The right paper style for the date range on these bills?"

"Perfect. But they've never been used," Wolfe said.

"And they were scheduled for destruction?" Bolan asked.

"You think the originals might have been destroyed?" Wolfe asked.

"It's not impossible. The retired printing machinery might have been acquired by someone else to make these bills," Bolan stated. "And they could have printed up this cash using the discard list."

"That's an awful lot of work for ten thousand dollars," Wolfe mused.

"Ten thousand in this stack, for this deal," Bolan noted. "How out of date are those bills?"

"Twenty years old," Wolfe told him. She chewed her lower lip. "So you're saying the machinery that printed these notes has been used for at least twenty years?"

"What cheaper way to finance a black-bag operation than to print your own cash?" Bolan asked. "Especially if you're using the money overseas. Ten thousand a mission, give it about eighteen missions a year," he said.

"Three point six million, minimum," Wolfe said. "Not counting local bribes, tickets, accommodations…"

"Paying for backup," Bolan added. "Let's call it five million in funny money. Officially printed on retired U.S. Treasury machinery. For a black-bag operation, it'd be obscenely cost-effective."

"That's just one operative," Wolfe noted. "How many organizations have only one top spook?"

Bolan nodded. "They'd be given similar budgets."

His cell phone warbled and he plucked it from his pocket. "Cooper."

"Striker," Hal Brognola's voice greeted him on the other side. "We have a possible incident in Phoenix involving our quarry."

"So he did get on a flight at LAX," Bolan noted.

"It's likely. We have an unknown body at the airport food court," Brognola said. "I've got local FBI agents running his fingerprints, but they couldn't get any."

"Just like our shooter," Bolan told the man from Justice. "The guy removed his fingerprints. We got tip impressions, but no identifiable markings on the bills or the wrapper."

"So we're talking about a serious covert operation," Brognola said.

"That's what Wolfe's thinking. They're using authentic printing machinery and supplies to cook up their own cash for their operations," Bolan said.

"Damn," Brognola grumbled. Bolan could hear his friend gnawing at the end of his cigar on the other end of the line.

"Can you get me to Phoenix?" Bolan asked.

"Chances are that our killer's flown the coop," Brognola stated.

"It'd get me closer to him," Bolan said. "I might be able to figure something out."

"Jack's just landed at LAX. With the Gulfstream, you could fly to Moscow if you wanted," Brognola said. "Granted, I hope you don't have to."

Bolan glanced through the window of Wolfe's lab, seeing four men in dark suits and sunglasses get off an elevator. They had visitor badges, and U.S. Treasury IDs hanging from their suit lapels.

"Jo, did the Treasury Department say anything about sending someone over to pick up the cash you ran through their listing?" Bolan asked.

Wolfe looked up from the money. "No. In fact they only wanted me to keep a couple bills for them. The rest I was told to break down for chemical composition testing. As long as I gave them the results—"

"Get down!" Bolan snapped.

The four men spotted the Executioner and his crime lab compatriot, and pulled submachine guns out from under their jackets. The only T-men Bolan knew who carried compact subguns were the Secret Service agents assigned to presidential protection details. Four counterfeiting investigators wouldn't require that kind of firepower, especially when paying a visit to the LAPD.

Bolan lunged across the table and knocked Wolfe to the floor an instant before the safety glass of the lab blew into translucent chunks. Wolfe grimaced, Bolan's weight crushing down on her for only an instant before he rolled off. The Desert Eagle filled his hand and he snapped off the safety with practiced skill.

Wolfe pulled her sidearm from her own holster, a .45-caliber Glock 30.

"Stay down," Bolan snarled. Whoever the gunmen were, they were disciplined. The streams of autofire were relentless, meaning that they were staggering their bursts, allowing their partners to reload.

Bolan guessed the position of the elevator through the low aluminum wall. At least one hose of 9 mm autofire came from that direction and the Executioner triggered his Desert Eagle, burning off the massive handgun's .44 Magnum payload. A scream of agony and a stutter in the constant cacophony of automatic weapon fire rewarded Bolan as the 240-grain slugs punched through the slim metal skin of the lab.

"Bastards toasted my microscope," Wolfe snarled. "I want a piece of them."

"I get first crack. If they somehow get past me, they're all yours," Bolan replied. He dumped the partially spent magazine and fed it a fresh stick.

"Hand over the cash and no one gets hurt!" came a bellow. Bolan grabbed a stool and swung it up through the shattered window. Uzi fire rattled, perforating the vinyl-clad seat. The angle betrayed the shooter's position and Bolan popped up. The front sight of the Desert Eagle locked on the Uzi-packing fake Fed. A single .44-caliber round slammed the gunman in the chest, hurling him to the floor. Bolan swiveled and saw a third gunman line up on him.

More thunderbolts ripped from the Desert Eagle, but the raider dived back into the elevator.

Wolfe lunged and shouldered Bolan to the floor as another rattling snarl of gunfire swept through the window. She grunted, spinning and clutching her shattered shoulder.

"He's still kicking," the scientist rasped as she tried to control the bleeding.

"Body armor," Bolan mused.

"Head shot," she suggested.

Bolan didn't waste the breath to let her know how obvious the advice was. He sighted on the perforated low wall and saw the flicker of movement through the bullet holes torn by the fake T-man. The Desert Eagle hammered out a rumbling thunderstorm of heavy slugs. Four rounds smashed through the sievelike wall panel, blowing it over. On the other side, the Uzi-packing man slumped lifeless, half of his face ripped off by a wide-mouthed hollowpoint round. The gun lay silenced between splayed legs.

A cabinet shuddered as more submachine gun fire rattled from the direction of the elevator.

"My paperwork," Wolfe groaned. Her face was screwed up in pain. "Dammit, stop shooting my files!"

Bolan rose to his feet and aimed at the gunman he'd nailed in the legs. The man swung his Uzi and pulled the trigger, but the weapon was empty. The Executioner vaulted over the cabinet and the low wall, spearing through the window. The third and fourth shooters were nowhere to be seen. He saw the wounded gunman struggling to reload his Uzi, but Bolan kicked the weapon from his hands and smashed his heel against the man's jaw on the swing back. Lab staff members came running.

"Officers! Secure this man!" Bolan snapped. "Get a medic for CSI Wolfe!"

"They moved out that way," a technician said. She held the side of her face, a shredded strip of skin livid from where she'd been pistol-whipped with an Uzi. "There's a controlled access stairwell, but they shot the lock to shit."

"I'm on it. Someone get on the radio and tell everyone to keep out of these guys' way," Bolan ordered. "They don't care who they kill."

"And you?" the hurt tech asked.

"I keep them from killing," Bolan said, racing off toward the stairwell.

3

The Executioner heard the gunmen's thundering footsteps below him in the stairwell. Bolan took the flights fast and furious, hopping when he was halfway down and rolling along the walls to eat up his forward momentum and get turned around to take the next flight. He was almost to the second floor when he heard the emergency exit slam open one floor below.

Bolan swung around and saw a dark-suited fake Treasury agent swing up his machine pistol. He lurched backward. A stream of 9 mm slugs filled the air where his head had been only moments ago, plaster chewed out of the undersides of the stairs above his head. He aimed his Desert Eagle and spiked a quartet of .44 Magnum slugs at the shooter. There was a snarled curse of panic as the man retreated.

Bolan bounded down the final steps as he holstered the big handgun and pulled his shoulder-holstered Beretta. The two men, posing as federal agents, had infiltrated the Los Angeles Crime Lab in an effort to gain control of counterfeit cash that Bolan was investigating. The two had survived the initial conflict, and the Executioner was going to keep the pair from escaping.

At the bottom of the steps, he burst into an alley and spotted the pair piling into their car. The Executioner raised the Beretta and ripped off a 3-round burst that took out the rear window of the car. They had a driver waiting behind the wheel, and he gunned the engine, tires spewing smoke before they caught hold and pushed the car forward.

Hot pursuit time, Bolan mused as he charged the length of the alley, punching more rounds, this time ripping 9 mm bullets into the road by the tires. After two tribursts, the right rear tire of the sedan exploded violently, flopping on its rim. The right fender screeched, wailing as it was shredded on contact with the wall, pulled off course by the deflated ring of floppy rubber.

Gunshots tore through the rear window, automatic weapons in the hands of the fake Feds churning out slugs. Had the driver not been in a struggle to maintain control of the limping sedan, the gunmen could have nailed the Executioner as he charged after them. But rather than hit their target, autofire sprayed wildly. As it was, the sedan ground to a halt, the front bumper rammed into a telephone pole. The driver ground the stick shift, trying to get the car into Reverse.

Bolan fired again, sinking another burst through the rear window, and suddenly the two muzzle-flashes became one. Bolan ducked behind a large garbage bin and reloaded his Beretta, knowing that at full gallop, he couldn't have been certain of a direct, fight-stopping hit on one of his opponents. Rather, it was likely that the silent weapon needed recharging, or had jammed.

Sure enough, a handgun took up the slack of the quieted Uzi. Bolan took a moment as bullets hammered the garbage bin, drew and tapped off his Desert Eagle with a few deft movements. He swung around the side with the Beretta and the .44 Magnum pistol in each hand. The sedan lumbered relentlessly back toward him, the enemy driver trying to turn his car into a missile.

The Executioner's handguns blazed out thunderbolts of Magnum firepower and sputtering lightning jolts of 9 mm bursts, ripping a dozen slugs into the charging beast. Then he whirled and jammed himself in the walkway between two structures.

The sedan bulldozed past, hurtling the garbage bin onto its side with a thunderous crash.

"Luke! Don't stop shooting!" a voice cried from the dark car. The rear passenger door was visible to Bolan in the walkway, and he could see an Uzi-toting man kneeling on the backseat. Bolan raised his Desert Eagle and fired twice. The second bullet was insurance in case the window deflected the first shot, but both Magnum slugs detonated gory holes through the gunner's back, sprawling him across his wounded partner.

"Stop the car!" Bolan shouted.

The driver leaned back to the rear of the car, leveled a pistol and opened fire. Bolan hit the sidewalk as slugs ripped into the brick around him, knocking loose explosions of stone splinters that rained down on him.

The sedan lurched forward, mangled metal chewing at the front tire, but the driver managed to wrestle some speed out of the damaged car.

Bolan burst into the alley and continued the chase as the enemy driver urged his wheels along. Wrecked as it was by impacts and tire-shredding bullets, the automotive dinosaur finally slowed enough to make foot pursuit possible.

But the driver suddenly jammed the car crosswise at the end of the alley, forming a barrier. The two survivors got out. One was hobbled by a bullet wound that had torn a chunk of muscle out of his thigh. The driver hooked his arm under the wounded man's and lurched into the street, aiming his handgun at the windshield of a passing SUV.

Bolan reached the alley's end and vaulted over the car, just as the driver deposited his wounded partner into the SUV. On the ground a woman, her chest bloody, gasped as she clutched the spreading dark smear. The Executioner stopped long enough to see if there was anyone else in the vehicle who could be a hostage. Bolan's pause to ensure the safety of innocents provided time for the fleeing driver to swing his pistol around and open fire. The driver blazed away at the Executioner and forced him to race in a serpentine charge for the nearest available cover. Bullets smashed the concrete at Bolan's heels.

The Executioner fired at the grille of the stolen SUV, hoping his Desert Eagle would have enough punch to render the massive V-8 engine useless to the escaping murderers. If he could force the pair into retreat, he could check on the woman and apply emergency first aid.

The driver was a wily, quick snake, however, diving into the seat well and jamming on the gas with his hand. The SUV lurched and rocketed down the street.

Bolan raced to the wounded woman.

"Can you talk?" he asked.

She winced, and blood trickled from her nose. The right side of her chest showed a ragged laceration, indicative of a glancing wound through her upper chest. The bullet went in, but had deflected off a rib bone and exited the side of her chest, slashing across her biceps. It was a grisly injury, but survivable. A closer examination showed that her nose was swollen from a brutal impact. Bolan was relieved to see that the nasal trickle wasn't bright red as if from an injured lung.

Bolan looked at the SUV as it disappeared into the distance.

A trio of LAPD squad cars screeched to a halt. The Executioner had his Justice Department badge around his neck, but he still held his hands up as the cops got out.

"Agent Cooper, FBI!" he announced. "Get this woman an ambulance."

HENRY COSTELL PICKED UP Cameron Richards in a nondescript, rusted old van. Richards didn't have to ask if his pilot and wheelman made certain that the vehicle was clean of any tracers or identifying features.

"Los Angeles was a screw job, Hank," Richards explained. "I think I was set up for a fall."

"It means they'll want to retire me and the others, too," Costell said. His close-cropped blond hair was a fuzz on top of his round, big-eared head.

"I can't believe that after all we've given them…" Richards said. He took a deep breath, putting the frustration away for later. "I've saved this country from countless threats."

"You've saved the whole world," Costell explained. "It doesn't matter. The weaklings in government aren't strong enough to do what has to be done against the hordes hemorrhaging through our southern border, or the maniacs in the Middle East."

"Don't even get me started on some of the shit we've seen in China," Richards whispered. "Hell, we've seen so many things that could destroy the world that we wouldn't have to look far." He paused for a moment.

"Why not?" Richards asked.

"Why not what?" Costell asked. "Destroy everything we've worked for?"

"We know enough to destroy the puppet masters," Richards said. "The ones who've been pulling our strings, the ones who've been pulling the strings of our enemies. We could take out the whole set of them, maybe give this world another chance."

Costell pulled into a parking lot and turned off the engine. "They'll kill us, no matter what we do," he admitted.

"This way, we not only give ourselves a measure of vengeance, but we create a new world. A world where people can live like they were meant to, by their own wits and courage," Richards said.

"There'd be battles across the country, not to mention international conflicts. And all we have is Weist and his men on our side," Costell countered.

"Not just him. We've got tabs on dozens of groups who would jump at the chance to play with the toys we're going to pull out of the chest," Richards stated. "We could build an army."

Costell stared, unfocused, out of the windshield. He didn't see the storefronts before him, but instead he saw a world that could be forged in the fires of a single act of apocalyptic revenge. He glanced back to Richards. "What would we use?"

"We've got everything from the Rage Pulse to Blue Fire," Richards answered.

"That stuff is under lock and key. The Initiative wouldn't let us touch it when we still were their trusted soldiers," Costell said.

"So what?" Richards asked. "We know where we can get it. They might have had contingencies for us, but we've got our own ideas."

"You're not really paranoid if they are out to get you,"

Costell agreed. "So we bust in, and pop off some doomsday weaponry."

"And if we're lucky, we can survive," Richards said. "But if not, we at least hit the real bastards."

"We'll need transportation," Costell noted.

"First we call up Weist and his boys," Richards said. "I've got some ideas for a ride that will get us exactly where we want to be."

4

Arnold Dozier didn't speak as Bolan entered the interrogation room. The Executioner simply stood there staring at the man he'd captured in the crime lab raid.

"So, what's your plan?" Dozier asked. "How're you going to break me?"

Bolan leaned over the table and opened the handcuffs connecting Dozier to the mooring pipe on the table. Dozier looked at the loosened fetters, then rubbed his wrist. He'd received some bruising from the LAPD cops who'd walked him in there, but nothing that couldn't be put down to Dozier's own clumsiness.

"I've got nothing on you," Bolan said. "You're a free man."

"Really?" Dozier asked.

"Apparently you don't exist," Bolan replied. He tossed the fingerprint chart on the table. "Arnold Dozier died ten years ago. And frankly, I don't have any known jurisdiction over the reanimated dead."

Dozier sneered. "You're kidding, right?"

"Nope," Bolan said. "Blow."

Dozier looked at the fingerprint chart in front of him.

His prints had been run and had come back as those of a dead man. He suddenly realized that Bolan and the LAPD had a list of paperwork on him. Photos, prints, and even if it all led to a dead end, the Rose Initiative wasn't going to take a breach of operational security lightly.

The big man turned and opened the door. Dozier looked past him and saw a row of grim-faced lawmen, some tightening grips on batons, others flexing their fingers through gleaming brass knuckles.

"So what's that?" Dozier asked.

"You're dead. You shouldn't worry about that," Bolan said. "Now blow."

Dozier knew the cops were waiting for their chance to give him some payback for the attack on their crime lab. "Why didn't you ask anything?" he said.

"Frankly, I don't have the time," Bolan answered. "You're obviously inured to interrogation techniques. Torture, drugs, sensory deprivation."

"But everyone breaks eventually," Dozier said.

"And while I'm doing that, the rest of your organization continues its operation, killing innocent American citizens," Bolan countered. "I'd spend the time to break you at the cost of what, thirty? A hundred? A thousand lives? Nah. I'll just let you go as a goat. When your friends pop up to eliminate you, I pounce on them. I work up the food chain. A worm to catch a small fish. A small fish to catch a big fish. A big fish to catch the shark."

Dozier shook his head. "They'll know I didn't talk."

"Like you just said—everyone breaks. Especially after the beating you'll take from my friends," the Executioner said.

Dozier frowned. He reached for the handcuffs. "I've got rights."

Dozier's head bounced from the force of Bolan's fist, and he sprawled across the floor.

"I told you, you have no rights. You're a dead man," Bolan stated. "Now get out of here."

Dozier looked at the gauntlet he'd have to run. He knew the big man was right. There was someone out there who would eliminate him. He struggled to sit in the chair, holding on to the restraint bar. "I'm staying," he said quietly.

Bolan's next punch rocked Dozier's head.

"Ask something!" Dozier snapped, thick, blood-filled spittle spraying all over Bolan's pants.

"It'll be a dead end," Bolan replied. "Now go."

Blood dripped from Dozier's mouth. "We're government. Not Treasury. We're called the Rose Initiative," he said.

"Never heard of it," Bolan said.

"Rose Initiative," Dozier repeated.

He regarded the Executioner. This was a man used to violence. He could see the hardness in his expression, the streaks of scar tissue on his skin. His very stance was one of restrained, explosive violence. But except for a few love taps, Dozier was unharmed.

"I told you, that name means nothing to me," Bolan replied. "Maybe if you make it mean something, I won't hang you out on the street as bait."

"The Rose Initiative is a semiofficial entity. We've had the blessing of various administrations since the fifties," Dozier said. "But we don't officially exist. Not on paper. Any sanction we get is merely implied."

"This way if you get caught, you can be denied—operating outside of government policy," Bolan surmised.

Dozier nodded.

"Who do you report to?" Bolan asked.

"Nobody official," Dozier said. "We're in the cold."

Bolan frowned. "But still close enough to the warmth to get legitimate T-man badges."

Dozier shrugged. He winced at the simple motion, remembering how the big man had used enough leverage to almost pop his shoulder out of shape.

"Who told you about the money at the crime lab?" Bolan asked.

"It came up on a computer watch," Dozier answered.

Bolan nodded.

Dozier wiped blood from his mouth. "I don't have anything on the upper levels of management. I'm just a grunt."

"Who's your immediate superior?"

"Winslow Spelling's about the only one I can assume is still out and around. He came with us as our driver, and the man's a snake," Dozier said.

"Where does this snake have his nest?" Bolan asked.

Dozier rattled off the name of a hotel and room number. "If he's still there."

"So why did you come after the money?" Bolan pressed.

"To cover up our involvement with the renegade," Dozier admitted.

"The assassin went rogue?" Bolan asked.

"Killed his handler at LAX. He's officially off the reservation," Dozier said. "We're trying to burn any leads back to us."

"So who's your rogue?" Bolan asked.

Dozier winced. "Cameron Richards."

"Identifying features?"

Dozier shook his head. "The man's a complete chameleon. It's why we picked him, because he can disappear in a crowd."

"He didn't disappear yesterday. He went through the crowd like a chain saw," Bolan growled.

"He might be off his medication," Dozier mused.

Bolan tilted his head.

"Mood suppressants keep him malleable enough for our purposes, yet leave him lucid enough to be a top line operative," Dozier explained. "Richards was a washout from special operations. His whole team is. Too violent, too ready to buy into whatever holy crusade. Richards was a true believer, and we milked his psyche to take advantage of that."

"So why Amanijad?" Bolan asked.

"Discrediting the hard-core factions. We wanted it to look like one of the radical right decided to begin the second Civil War early," Dozier said.

"Second Civil War?" Bolan asked.

Dozier nodded. "From the ashes of modern corrupt society, a new phoenix will rise. That's the joke of the Initiative's name. We've already risen."

Bolan's eyes narrowed.

"Richards has taken on real threats as well. But he's still convinced that the union will shatter again. And this time, the rift won't be healed," Dozier said.

"You're cultivating this?" Bolan asked.

"No. A little tension is good. It keeps the attention off us while we do what we have to," Dozier explained. "The problem is that some of the hard right have been…examining some of our roots. Conspiracy theorists who in their quest to find the New World Order were sniffing too close to our home."

"And for that, dozens of innocent people had to be killed and wounded?" Bolan asked.

Dozier nodded. "Corpses made by our enemies create excellent distractions."

"Then you're going to love this, Dozier," Bolan said. He turned toward the open the door.

"What are you doing?" Dozier asked.

"Walking out. You can go run to the Rose Initiative, and you can tell them I'm on their trail," Bolan explained.

"What?"

"You think I'm going to give my word of honor to a liar and a murderer? Get real. I've got what I wanted," Bolan told him. "You are the purest form of scum I've dedicated my life to destroying."

"The Rose Initiative will kill me!" Dozier cried.

"Someone should," Bolan said. He closed and locked the door behind him.

Brognola would have someone take care of the venomous thug.

ALLISON CALLAHAN WAS a classically beautiful woman. She had thick, lustrous strawberry-blond hair and a curvaceous figure, and Bolan could see a keen, calculating intellect behind her sparkling hazel eyes. She examined Bolan as if he were a slide subject under a microscope. She held out her hand and he took it. Her grip was firm.

It made sense. As a forensic scientist, Callahan had developed a handshake that was cop-proof. She had to have expected Bolan to come forward with a knuckle-grinding grasp. Her smile was all the evidence the Executioner needed to ascertain the truth of his suspicion.

"You must be Agent Matt Cooper," Callahan said. She eyed his knuckles. "Been having a rough day."

"Chasing down the thugs who attacked the crime lab," Bolan said.

Callahan looked him in the eyes. She wasn't convinced

by Bolan's explanation. The bruises on his strong, callused hands were too livid to be anything other than fresh.

"Having a talk with one of them," Bolan added.

Callahan nodded. "He most likely deserved everything you gave him."

"He'll be regretting his decision for a while," Bolan said.

She looked questioningly at him, but the Executioner's cold gaze informed her that the subject was closed.

"What have you got for me on the three you got to see?" Bolan asked.

"We're running checks on them now," Callahan stated. "The coroner examined their stomach contents, thinking we could narrow down where they were before they launched the raid."

"Any luck with that?" Bolan asked.

"I was going down to trace to check it out. Feel up to looking through vomit?" Callahan asked.

Bolan shrugged. "I've done worse."

The corner of Callahan's mouth rose slightly. Bolan could tell she was feeling him out, to see if he was worth working with. He knew that too often, when a cop was hooked up with a federal agent, there was a quick contest of wills.

Sifting through the partially digested last meals of three men he'd killed was undoubtedly a test of Bolan's mettle.

As they entered the trace lab, Bolan looked at the three pans filled with bile and chunks of food. Callahan handed Bolan a box of latex gloves, and he donned a pair.

"Looks like Mexican food at first blush," Bolan said. He leaned forward and took a whiff of the contents of one tray. "Hard to pin down the exact kind, though. The stomach acid's altered the smell. Might be El Salvadoran or even something farther south."

Callahan nodded in approval. "Some of the spices we've found are indicative of Honduran cuisine. It narrows things down significantly, as the Honduran community is fairly compact."

Bolan took his note with the hotel listing given to him by Dozier and compared it with a map that Callahan had placed on the light table. "This last known address also fits with the area. We might not have an exact restaurant, but we do have someplace to look."

"I've also had some of the other crime-lab staff go over the tires of the vehicle left in the alley. We've got soil samples, and signs of fresh tar in some of the treads," Callahan added.

"Repaving? Or was it just loose pellets dropped in a pothole that didn't melt together?" Bolan inquired.

Callahan's smile widened. "So the super Fed knows his way around an investigation."

"Not my specialty, but observation has always been a skill of mine," Bolan answered. "I pass your test?"

Callahan nodded. "Yeah. You're in my cool book. And yes, unlike most people, I really do have a book of cool people."

Bolan nodded. "Thanks for the heads-up. I'll take a trip over to the neighborhood and see if anything's popped up."

"By yourself?" Callahan asked.

Bolan nodded.

"You'll at least need backup," Callahan offered.

"Jo Wolfe got shot today hanging out too close to me," Bolan countered. "Don't worry. I'll be back. I want to see if you manage to pick up anything else about these men."

Callahan looked skeptical.

"These men were part of a supposedly top-secret project. Look close to see if they have any special immunizations or radioactive trace elements in their blood-stream," Bolan said. "The sooner I spread this investigation out of the Los Angeles area, the better chance I have of finding out where my quarry's off to."

"The Hondurans aren't going to just roll over for you," Callahan warned.

Bolan wasn't fazed. "By the time I'm finished with them, they'll come to heel."

COLONEL JACOB WEIST LOWERED his binoculars, then glanced over to Richards and Costell.

"You mean to tell me that we're going to break into one of the most highly defended installations in this country and fly out with advanced, high-tech helicopters?" Weist asked.

Richards nodded. "Pretty much."

Weist grinned and scanned the horizon. "The base layout is fairly generic. We could make the most effective equipment retrieval with a Delta Seven assault pattern, given the troops I have with me."

Richards agreed with a slight grunt. "That's what I was figuring too."

Weist let the binoculars hang on their strap. "I can't believe the Initiative tried to make you into a scapegoat."

"It's not so much that," Richards replied. "I've been looking online, and the blame seems to be resting on our fellow true believers. The cover story for my op was changed, and now the last people in America who actually remember her purity and ideals are coming under blame for my so-called terrorist attack on Los Angeles."

"They tried to kill you, though," Weist said.

"No, they noticed that Cam was no longer under their chemical leash when he reported to his liaison," Costell said. "With those drugs still running in our system, we wouldn't think to look if the right people were taking the blame for the death of that anti-American Arab."

Weist shook his head. "I knew it was too much of a good thing to be paid by the government to fight the important battles."

"I'm just glad we pulled you off of your coyote patrol," Richards noted. "We need good men. All the good we can find."

"You have us," Weist responded. "We can stem the tide of illegals across our border anytime. But when our own leadership betrays us…"

Weist grimaced. "I can barely believe it. But ever since we stopped taking our vitamins, you're right. Everything is clearer. I'm no longer in the same haze I used to be."

"You're asking questions," Richards explained. "The pills, they nullified our ability to reason, without hindering our tactical abilities."

Weist's eyes narrowed. "We can use the advanced X-birds in that facility to give us all the advantage we need against our enemies."

"We're not going to run," Richards said. "We're going to take the fight to them. But if we take down the Rose Initiative and the traitors they prop up, then we're leaving our nation open to our enemies."

Weist looked askance. "Not only that, but if we take down the puppeteers, the country will turn against itself. It'll be a civil war again."

"A civil war, war with China, the mullahs and the Mexicans hitting the disparate parties," Richards said. "Apocalypse in a bag."

"So what do we do?" Weist asked.

"We get those choppers, and we get to some truly nasty weaponry," Richards said.

"The Extinction Archive!" Weist exclaimed.

"None other," Richards confirmed. "From there, we can easily take out any opposition, including China."

Weist rolled it over in his mind, and he nodded. "Fuck all of them before they fuck us again."

Richards smiled, looking at the base. "How long before we make our move?"

"Give me two hours," Weist said.

"Two hours," Richards repeated. "Two hours, and the first step in freeing this country will be taken."

5

The Executioner moved easily, slipping into the shadows of the alley. He grimaced as he mentally reviewed his war load, concerned about the implications of using too much firepower in the middle of Los Angeles. With his signature pistols riding under one arm and on his right hip and a sound-suppressed assault carbine in a gym bag, he had enough firepower to take on a company of enemy soldiers, and yet, only a few blocks back, children sat on a curb, fiddling with tiny electronic toys in their chubby little palms.

The building he was closing in on used to be an old machine shop, but an arm twisted here, and a leg broken there, informed him that it was a refuge for members of the Honduran immigrant community who could find easy profit in black market weapons and illicit narcotics. Bolan knew if something went wrong, he would drop a war in the middle of a civilian population. Unlike Richards, the rogue government assassin he sought, there was nothing in the Executioner's heart of hearts that could allow a battle plan that turned unarmed bystanders into targets. And yet, except for targeting those who weren't part of the battle, Richards's extraction plan resembled the kind of hit and run blows against enemy governments that the Executioner specialized in.

Though he and Richards paralleled each other tactically, ethically they were polar opposites. Richards saw his duty to his government as a license to kill without restraint. Bolan was obligated to his duty to justice, which meant that the only ones who should suffer directly by his hand were the predators who inflicted their own suffering.

The smell of gunpowder was strong as Bolan closed in on the machine shop. A burly, bullet-headed man stood guard, the ugly outline of a heavy handgun bulging against his washboard stomach as he leaned against the back door. Cruel, dark eyes scanned the alley as Bolan nestled in the doorway, observing him.

The door guard was a hardened professional thug, observant and obviously quick. Only Bolan's stealth and the lowering of the sun in the sky, extending shadows, gave him an element of surprise. Bolan set down his war bag containing his collapsed assault carbine and stepped out of the shadows. He had his Beretta shielded from view behind his leg, and the alley was empty enough that a stray shot wouldn't end up in a noncombatant.

The tough guy saw Bolan and didn't even offer a vocal challenge. His instincts were good, and his hand dived to the pistol-butt poking out of his waistband. With the Beretta already in hand, the Executioner had the advantage, snapping it up and punching a sound-suppressed bullet through the bridge of the gang member's nose. The 9 mm slug drilled through bone and brain, and lifeless fingers dropped the thick, ugly pistol in his hand.

Bolan turned back and scooped up his rifle, pulling it from its concealing case. This wasn't going to be a soft probe, but the quiet approach had already been risked. The moments before the contraband runners discovered that they were under attack were falling away quickly, the countdown to a full-fledged conflict was evaporating like alcohol under a blow torch. He strode swiftly up to the door the thug had been guarding, and pulled the trigger on the Masterkey shotgun under the barrel of his carbine. The "key to any door" was a 12-gauge chunk of enamel-fused lead filings weighing an ounce, a hybrid slug of metal and polymer that disintegrated on contact with a lock, but in the process rendered the lock useless. A blunt gas collecting canister on the nose of the Masterkey muffled the thunder of the shotgun's bellowing report, but the door still slammed open violently, its clatter alerting a pair of men looking over an open crate of hand grenades.

The handguns jammed into their belts informed Bolan that they weren't choir boys, and the Executioner milked the trigger on his folding stock VEPR, the stubby suppressor swallowing most of the chatter of the American-made AK-47 as its 7.62 mm COMBLOC rounds ripped into one heavily tattooed gang member as his hand dropped to the pistol at his side. The other one gawped at the Executioner in stunned shock, so Bolan reversed the VEPR and smashed its tube-steel buttstock hard into the man's chin, knocking him senseless. He relieved the prisoner of his handgun.

Bolan rested his foot on the stunned man's thigh and replaced the VEPR with the huge, gleaming Desert Eagle. The big .44 Magnum pistol was pure intimidation. The big American addressed the dazed arms inspector in Spanish.

"You sold some Uzis to a group of white men," Bolan said. "Where are they now?"

"I don't know anything about that," the gang member answered.

The blocky muzzle of the Desert Eagle crashed across the man's cheek, splitting skin and laying bone bare. "Who would?"

"Armageddo," the wounded man grunted.

"He in the building?" Bolan asked.

"Next room," the Hispanic answered.

"What does he look like?"

"He has devil horns tattooed on his forehead. Bright red, amid the crown of thorns," the gang member stated.

A second swipe of the big Magnum's barrel to the temple left Bolan's captive unconscious on the floor.

"What the fuck is the noise in here?" someone cursed, opening the door, gun leading.

Bolan checked for the devil horns, then pulled the trigger on the Desert Eagle, spearing the hapless man back through the doorway, a gaping hole in the center of his face.

The Executioner burst into Armageddo's workplace as the arms dealers were still gawking in shock at their dead partner thrown to the floor. Bolan was in the room among them, even as the corpse flopped on the floor tiles, transitioning from the Desert Eagle to the folding-stock rifle. The gang members scrambled in wild panic as the heavily armed Executioner exploded into action.

The men going for shotguns and rifles around the room were his first targets, though Bolan paused in his sweep of the autorifle's muzzle to check for the devil-horns of Armageddo. Everyone who didn't display their satanic adornments caught a burst of suppressed AK fire, heavy-caliber slugs shredding flesh and splintering bone with lethal authority.

The panic and scrambled recovery bought Bolan three seconds, and four more corpses littered the floor of the machine shop turned arms bazaar. Instead of reacting to battle, Armageddo and two burly thugs sought cover. Bolan chased one of the two bodyguards with a quick rip from his VEPR. He heard a pained cry as his bullet carved a furrow in the man's calf.

The minor injury bought the Executioner a free shot at the bodyguard as he popped up, swinging a Desert Eagle of his own. The .50-caliber handgun bellowed before the goon could align his sights, firing wildly, instead of concentrating on aim, or at least good shooting form. Had the gunman been braced with the muzzle aligned on target, Bolan would have felt the searing agony of 300 grains of lead sizzling through his chest. Instead, he saw a muzzle-flash and the barrel whip toward the ceiling under a powerful recoil. Bolan, however, had his rifle tucked to his shoulder, and tripped the trigger only when the front sight was locked on the shooter's shoulder. Bolan's two rounds lanced through flesh and bone, cracking the joint apart and tossing the stunned arms dealer to the floor.

Armageddo cursed loudly, ordering his remaining bodyguard to turn the Executioner into hamburger.

"Fuck that" was the response. The bodyguard raced toward a boarded-over window and hurled himself at the plywood sheet. Nails tore loose and wood splintered as the man chose discretion over valor. Seeing six of his brethren taken down in the space of a few seconds had obviously informed the bodyguard that sticking around was suicide.

"Where's Spelling, Armageddo?" Bolan asked, working a fresh magazine into his VEPR.

"The hell if I tell you," the gang lord answered. He poked his Glock over the top of a crate and pulled the trigger, firing blindly. The shots came nowhere close to the Executioner. Bolan checked his aim and fired a round from the shotgun through the box that Armageddo hid behind.

A vomitous eruption of splinters and hay gushed near

Armageddo's side, the box cored by an ounce of bonded lead and polymer. Against anything short of a steel lock, it was like a hot knife through butter. Bolan made sure the blast was close enough to make the man sweat and realize that nothing in a machine shop was cover against the firepower he carried.

"Drop the piece and tell me where Spelling is, or I make you a paraplegic," Bolan warned. "You show up in Lompoc Federal Penitentiary without the use of your legs, you'll be the prettiest girl at the dance."

The Glock toppled from Armageddo's fingers, clattering atop the crate.

"Spelling," Bolan repeated.

"He called me for a pickup. Said he needed to get to an airport," Armageddo said. "He's got a midnight flight."

"Stand up," Bolan ordered.

The man did so.

"Which airport?" Bolan asked.

Armageddo told him.

Bolan nodded. "You've got two bodies to drag out of here to safety before I burn down this festering wound."

Armageddo raised an eyebrow, then saw Bolan pull a radio-detonator-equipped packet of C-4 and thermite powder from his web belt. He backed away, but the VEPR was leveled at the gang leader's gut.

"You run, I spray paint the merchandise with your bowels. Grab your survivors and take them to safety," Bolan said. "You've got a message to deliver. Your group is out of business. Start again, and I'll make sure it's permanent next time."

The crime boss went to his wounded bodyguard and picked him up in a fireman carry. Bolan waited until he returned to pick up the thug that he'd left unconscious in the back room, then set his charge.

Armageddo watched as Bolan strode past him, ignoring him as he exited the alley. One thumb of the detonator and the machine shop turned arms bazaar disappeared in a stone-crumpling explosion.

Armageddo turned and ran like a frightened child.

ANDERSON SIGHED AS HE STEPPED into the gate guard booth. With a chamber-empty Beretta on his hip, the deadliest thing near him was the bottle of liquor in the bottom drawer of the desk. It was going to be a long slow night. Not that he minded. He had a thick book of crossword puzzles, the bottle of booze and a pack of cigarettes somewhere.

He chuckled, mentally correcting himself about the deadliest thing in the guard booth. It wasn't the empty handgun. It was the damned cancer sticks. He sighed, and shuffled around in the drawer for one anyway. He couldn't help it; he had the nicotine monkey on his back. As he rose and looked over the lower edge of the guardhouse window, he saw the muzzle of a handgun aimed at him.

"Hey, careful. That might actually be loaded," the MP said with a chuckle.

"It is," Cameron Richards whispered. He pulled the trigger on the Beretta and blew Anderson's brains out of the back of his head.

Weist and Costell drove the troop truck through the gates as Richards hit the controls, standing astride the MP's corpse. A team of highly trained commandos was in the back of the truck, laden with loaded and ready weapons, unlike the lamebrains who were assigned to protecting the XH-92 stealth helicopters.

Richards bent and plucked the corpse's Beretta from its holster. He checked the magazine well and the chamber, finding them both empty. He sighed and dropped the useless weapon and dug around for the man's spare magazines. He found none and shook his head in disgust. He set a wad of C-4 under the desk and then hurried to catch up with the truck.

One of Weist's commandos reached out and helped Richards into the back of the truck.

"When are they going to learn that this nation is at war?" Richards growled. "The guard at the gate had an unloaded handgun and no magazines."

"It's the damned liberals," the trooper replied. "They don't want anyone armed. Not even their own troops."

"Just the bodyguards their ass-kissing money gets them," another of Weist's men added. "They can have all the guns they want."

"Whatever," Richards grumbled. "We're not taking those helicopters a moment too soon. If this is what our military has dissolved into, fucking crossing guards with paperweights on their hips, then we need to act now."

"We're on our way," the first commando said. "We're going to make everything right."

Richards nodded as the truck crawled down the road, closing on the hangar. Since the XH-92 was a top-secret program, it was in a recessed blockhouse built into the side of the mountain, keeping it safe from spy satellites and potential bombing runs from enemy governments. And for all that security, Richards bitterly noted, they still had unarmed gate guards.

He shook his head, then hung out over the tailgate, scanning the road ahead. If they were lucky, the rest of the guard force would be equally lax. If not, well, the detonation of the gate and the road mines tossed out in the wake of the transport trucks would provide enough confusion and distraction for them to get their job done.

"READER, WHAT'S WRONG?" Colonel Nelson Storm asked as he walked up to the slender scientist who stood in the doorway of the hangar, looking intently out over the tarmac.

"Is someone throwing things out of the back of that troop truck?" Reader asked.

Storm squinted. He cursed himself for not letting his eyes acclimate to the darkness, but instinct had him drop his hand to the pistol he had holstered on his hip. "I'll have to take your word for it, Doctor."

Reader glanced over. "I should get the other technicians out of the way."

"Good idea. Maybe keep your hand on that revolver you keep in your pocket holster too," Storm noted.

"Good idea," Reader said.

"Move it, Doctor," Storm ordered. He reached into his flap holster, pulling out his old Colt .45. He inserted a fresh magazine and cycled the slide to make the gun hot. It was a violation of safety regulations, but he wanted to be alive to be punished for a violation. Even now, he could see gallon-sized milk bottles bouncing over the tailgate of the truck racing toward the hangar.

There wasn't supposed to be a crew coming in to join the current team doing diagnostic tests of the XH-92 stealth helicopters. Added security was also out of the question. He would have received a heads-up in case there was a threat requiring an additional platoon.

"Okay, boys! Lock and load!" Storm shouted. "This is

the real fucking shit! I want your rifles hot and your peckers hard!"

The airmen who were working security on the hangar looked confused at first. Sergeant Emily Walters, however, was on the ball, slamming a magazine into the well of her M-16 and working its bolt.

Good girl, the veteran officer thought.

"What's the deal?" Walters asked.

"We've got a standard deuce and a half moving at a good clip up the road," Storm said. "They're littering like crazy, and no one's authorized to come up this road."

"Light her up?" Walters asked.

"At this range, that pussy little .22 won't even dent the hood," Storm growled. "Take Lumpkin and hunker down in that gully there. I want them in an effective cross fire. Cage, Crystal, on the door with me. And someone get me a fucking rifle!"

Reader jogged through the access door, carrying two M-16s. "You rang?"

"Doctor," Storm protested.

"I'm ex-military," Reader countered. "I'm familiar with a service rifle. And five against a truckload isn't going to be worth spit."

"So six will do better?" Storm asked.

"Twenty percent increase in firepower," Reader said, handing the M-16 to Storm.

"Fucking rocket scientists, always knowing the numbers," Storm grumbled. "Okay, Cage and Crystal, check your fire. Keep your arc between that light post and the boulder ten feet in front of the other's position. I'm setting up a cross fire, not putting us in a position where we'll be pouring bullets into each other. Walters,

Lumpkin—the end of your arc is where I'm standing right now. Doc, on me."

Storm led the scientist up the side of the hill.

"They'll have seen us setting up our positions, if they have night vision," Reader noted.

"It's still a defensible fire position. The defenders usually have the advantage," Storm said. "Are the other scientists okay?"

"I've ordered them into the underground vent tunnels. They won't stop until there's a whole mountain between them and the shit storm coming," Reader responded.

"You should be with them," Storm reminded the scientist. "This isn't your fight."

"Sorry, but the government paid me to make sure this helicopter can protect our country. Can't do that if it gets stolen," Reader said.

Storm sighed and nestled himself on a ledge of rock and sand. Reader set up position five yards to his right, laying prone and with the rifle in a tight cheek weld. Storm was glad to have a sixth rifleman on his side.

The colonel saw the flare of a rocket engine off the side of the approaching truck. He'd spent enough time in the Gulf being shot at with RPG rockets to know what was coming. With a surge of strength, he tossed himself off the rocky ledge, bellowing for Reader to follow him.

The scientist did follow Storm, but in pieces separated by the lethal thunderclap of the thermobaric RPG-7 warhead. Reader's half-skinned head landed in Storm's lap, and it took everything in the colonel's willpower to snap the M-16 to his shoulder. The first burst raised sparks on the truck's hood, but the vehicle kept hammering forward.

Another RPG shell leaped off the bed of the transport

truck. The attackers had sliced vents in the tarp and were leaning out through the improvised firing portals. The authoritative chug of a light machine gun opened up, sweeping across the hangar entrance. Storm knew that whatever cover Cage and Crystal were behind, it might not be enough to stop a 7.62 mm NATO fusillade. Sure enough, he heard only the rattle of one M-16 echoing in the arched hangar entrance. Storm triggered his rifle again, hoping that as the enemy vehicle drew closer, it would become more vulnerable to his own rifle's 5.56 mm rounds.

The concussion blast that erupted near him ended that hope as he was lifted up like a rag doll and hurled against the rocky cliff. His M-16 skidded down the slope, and he could tell that his right arm was broken in at least two places by the way it bent wildly. He stuck his good hand down and twisted his Colt .45 from its holster.

At least two good men were down. Maybe more. With a broken arm, he couldn't do much more than fumble with his handgun. He managed to twist the .45 to a firmer grasp and finger off the safety. The pistol barked its message, but the range was more than fifty yards, and firing with his bad hand, in the darkness, having been rocked by an RPG shell that broke his arm, he couldn't hit the broadside of a barn. He fired three shots, but enemy gunmen opened up with their rifles. Storm hauled himself behind a rock, tucking himself down. The thunderous blasts of autofire tore splinters of the rock, but Storm was protected.

They stopped shooting, but Storm was helpless. He was wounded, low on firepower and outnumbered significantly. The firefight had gone silent. The colonel lay on his back, gasping for breath and prayed. At least the technicians had made it out safely.

That's when Storm heard the rolling howl of the stealth helicopters. Both of them together hovered in the hangar entrance. They hung for a moment in the air, then the sound of their rotors disappeared, the slap turning into the rush of a stiff breeze. They floated like dragonflies for a moment, then rocketed off into the night sky. Along the road, the containers seen by Reader detonated, shattering the road, spikes of flame spitting up into the darkness. He saw the deadly aircraft disappear through the fires of hell.

6

Winslow Spelling looked in the mirror, checking his hair's dye job. He needed to change his appearance, and his blond locks were just too recognizable to the big man in black who chased him in Los Angeles. The Glock rested on the sink edge, close at hand. He put in a pair of contact lenses to change the color of his green eyes to brown.

He affixed a black mustache to his upper lip with spirit gum, then disguised the scent of the cosmetic adhesive with a splash of strong cologne. Spelling tucked in his shirt, then pushed the pistol into his waistband. It wouldn't take long for him to get to the airport and take a charter flight to a more secure location.

Spelling picked up his bag, then walked toward the door to the hotel room. He was about to turn the doorknob when the door exploded in his face. The edge cracked him across the nose and cheek hard enough to split skin. Blood poured from his broken nose, and he blinked, trying to clear his vision. Another impact landed in the middle of his forehead, snapping his head back like a gunshot. Spelling stumbled backward for a few steps before his balance disappeared and he collapsed, his bag tumbling from his fingers.

"Going somewhere?" the Executioner growled.

Spelling fumbled for the Glock in his waistband. Before he could get a secure grip, his testicles felt as if they were jammed up into his sternum from a savage kick. The handgun was forgotten as his legs folded up to his stomach for protection.

Bolan reached down and took the handgun from the stunned fake Fed.

Spelling gasped for breath. He thought about the handgun on his ankle, but Bolan grabbed Spelling's bent leg and hauled his foot up, ripping the small revolver out of its holster. A second kick to the genitals informed Spelling that his testicles were still down between his thighs, because they lanced a flame of agony up through his belly.

Spelling coughed, choking on his own bile. He could feel stomach acid in his nostrils. He spit out gobs of stinging vomit. The big man reached down and ran his fingers through Spelling's hair, then knotted them and pulled him up by his scalp.

"You're protecting Richards?" Bolan asked.

"Erasing the trail," Spelling croaked. "Make it easier to erase the mistake."

"A mistake," Bolan repeated.

Spelling nodded. "He's gone off his meds. He's loosed his leash, and he's acting under his programming."

"You programmed him that way?" Bolan asked. "Your sick little agency?"

"His father. He was raised in a trailer park," Spelling said. "Because the old shit couldn't keep a decent job, he blamed the Mexicans and the blacks for the fact he was an unemployed moron. The son of a bitch was relentless in drilling into Richards's head all kinds of poison shit."

Bolan pushed Spelling into a chair, looking the man in his teary eyes. "You recruited him?"

"Minimized the damage to my cousin," Spelling replied.

"I'd feel sorry for you, but you shot an innocent woman for her wheels," Bolan returned.

Spelling nodded, weeping.

"Your bosses won't appreciate this failure," Bolan said. "But I can arrange some safety for you."

"I just need to betray the Rose Initiative to you?" Spelling asked.

Bolan didn't answer. "You want to live, you take the risk. Otherwise, I leave you defenseless in a prison cell."

Spelling frowned.

Bolan sighed, then pulled a cell phone.

"Who're you calling?" Spelling asked.

"Justice Department. A team of marshals will be by to pick you up soon enough. I presume the Rose Initiative has its taps into them, right?" Bolan asked. "If they do, they might even have a chance to tear you to pieces good and slow."

Spelling sneered. His face hurt like hell, and the big man in black had him under the gun. He was offering a slim chance at survival, but that meant going up against the Initiative, a covert-operations juggernaut. Still, Spelling had watched the big man in action, and if anyone had a chance, it was him. "You have a doctor to fix up my face at least?"

Bolan folded the phone and put it away. "You cross me..."

"I'm dead," Spelling replied.

Bolan shook his head. "Why make things easy for you? Fighting the Initiative, you might luck out and go quick with a bullet. Anything else, I make sure the carrion feeders have a living meal to tear apart."

Spelling swallowed apprehensively.

"Just so we're clear," Bolan explained. "I want Richards. And if your people get in my way, good. Saves me the trouble of looking for them on my own."

"Who are you?" Spelling asked.

"Just another dead man, Spelling," Bolan said. "To you, I'm the devil, come to collect his due," the Executioner warned. "Not many get a chance to change their judgment, Spelling. Count yourself lucky."

Spelling nodded, chilled to the bone.

RICHARDS GAVE COSTELL A PAT on the shoulder as the XH-92 sliced through the night sky, heading toward their rendezvous.

"We got away with it," Costell muttered. "I am impressed."

"That's Weist," Richards responded.

"We drop you off in Idaho, and then fly nap of the Earth, avoiding interceptors until we reach Washington, D.C.," Costell said, remembering Richards's instructions. "You'll contact us via the dead drop phone."

"Right. I'll be bringing an army to distract the enemy," Richards noted. "Even with Weist and these helicopters, we're going to be hard-pressed to put one over on the traitors."

Costell glanced back at his friend. "We might actually stand a chance?"

"Whatever happens, live or die, we will no longer be puppets," Richards said. "Whether they kill us before we finish the job, or not, we'll have destroyed Washington and set hell in motion across the world."

Costell nodded, looking a little numb. "I just can't believe they fed us this crap. And we bought it."

"Our medication. They told us it was to prevent infection and radiation poisoning, but that was a lie. They didn't want us returning to question our actions," Richards said.

"How did you know?" Costell asked.

"There was another, someone who'd broken his programming in the first place," Richards explained.

"Another like you?" Costell asked.

Richards nodded. "They'd blinded me, making me think he was just some no-talent amateur. A loose cannon who needed removing. But he'd broken his programming. He captured me, tried to free me from the drugs."

Costell whistled. "That's great. He's on our side?"

"I killed him," Richards stated.

"Killed him?" Costell repeated.

"He was already brainwashed, which is why the medication didn't affect him. He believed in all of these socialist, society-killing causes, like allowing faggots to practice, integrating races, and dissent against the government."

"We're dissenting," Costell spoke up.

"No. We're in revolution against tyrants who have usurped the rightful constitution," Richards stated. "He was just some fanatic who believed in rebelling just because they were of a certain political slant."

"God damn it," Costell cursed.

"I know. We don't need people like him. He'd poison the next society that takes over," Richards replied.

"Good work," Costell complimented him. "We're closing in on the bus station. I'll drop you off a mile out, so no one sees this bird."

"Thanks," Richards said. "Be careful."

"You too," Costell answered.

Richards, having changed into civilian clothes during the flight, hopped to the back of the helicopter. He gave Costell a thumbs-up, then disappeared into the night.

BROGNOLA WATCHED AS THE MEDIC stitched together the huge rift that had been torn in Winslow Spelling's face. He frowned, glancing over to Mack Bolan who was checking out the gear meant for the new operative on his team.

"You're going to trust him with a loaded gun?" Brognola whispered.

"Better than leaving him as a walking target," Bolan said. "He knows he's expendable. He also knows that if he survives this, he's earned his freedom."

"Someone like him?" Brognola asked.

Bolan nodded. "It's not a perfect opportunity, but right now, he knows more about Richards than anyone."

"He's family," Brognola reminded Bolan.

"Family who he knew was damaged by a racist father," Bolan countered. "He thought that the Rose Initiative would make the most of his cousin's internal conflicts, giving him enough focus to do some good for society."

"And yet, he ends up being the worst that society can offer," Brognola stated. "We're trying to crack into the Rose Initiative's database. We're not finding much, since Spelling's access was cut off when he was late for his projected escape."

"It's enough of a handle for Bear and the team to penetrate their defenses," Bolan said. "They'll break the code."

"What we have found is an APB for Spelling, linking him to some heinous activity," Brognola continued. "Take a look."

Bolan glanced at the file set before him. Crime scene photos attributed to Spelling spread out like grisly wallpaper. The Executioner recognized some of the faces, and he suppressed a sneer, glancing toward Spelling.

"Put a bullet in his head and—" Brognola began. He caught the Executioner's cold glare and stopped.

"Keep your friends close, and your enemies closer,"

Bolan reminded Brognola. "That tactic has helped me survive all this time."

"I can think of a dozen times when that tactic had you tortured and nearly executed."

Bolan shrugged. "I never anticipated dying in my sleep, unless it was from unconsciousness induced by blood loss and trauma."

Spelling walked over, slipping his Glock into his waistband holster. "My ears are burning here."

Bolan looked at the livid line of stitches crossing the center of the turncoat's face. "It's not your imagination. My friend here says I'd be smart just to shoot you and dump you in a lye pit," he stated.

Spelling nodded. "You didn't recruit an angel, big man."

"No. But you will go by my rules now," the Executioner said. "First rule—there are no acceptable losses. You cause a civilian to die, you let a lawman go down, you get sent to a prison listed as a pedophile, and your broken pelvis will make you the easiest prey in the whole cell block."

Spelling shrugged. "Don't expect a miracle."

Bolan sighed, then pulled his Desert Eagle from its holster. With speed like quicksilver, he reversed the handgun and smashed the butt of the heavy pistol against the stitched bridge of Spelling's nose. The lightning-fast impact threw Spelling onto the ground. Stitches ruptured, and blood squirted in pulses from the re-opened injury. "Sorry, Doctor."

"No problem," the physician said. The man was one of Brognola's contacts who shared Bolan's ethics. "He doesn't need a renewal of his freeze, I'll just stitch it shut."

Spelling winced, fighting the urge to cry out as the needle and surgical thread pushed through ruptured skin. Without the numbing embrace of anesthetic, tears flushed from Spelling's eyes, but once the doctor was done, he didn't make another sound.

"If I expect you to walk on water, then you'd better well walk on water," Bolan said. "I can make your continued existence more hell than you ever imagined."

"Any more rules?" Spelling asked, wincing at the ferocity of the Executioner.

"Just the first rule," Bolan explained.

Spelling stood. "Then I'm ready."

Bolan nodded. "That's the spirit. You might just get your shot at redemption, Spelling."

The operative groaned, popping aspirin into his mouth and swallowing them dry.

SERGEANT EMILY WALTERS swallowed a pair of painkillers, then saw her nurse lead two figures into her hospital room.

"Agents Stone and Hutchinson," the nurse said, then turned and left.

"This another round of questions about the stolen choppers?" Walters asked, bitterness filling her tone. She looked at the pair. Both were big, strongly built men, both with black hair, though Hutchinson's looked like it was a dye job. Across the center of his face was a livid, freshly stitched scar. Stone looked as craggy as if he were hewn from his namesake material, but he also held the majesty of a mountain range.

"The thieves," Stone said. "Did you get a good look at them?"

Walters winced from the pain of the gunshots she'd received in her shoulder and arm, as well as broken ribs from where her body armor stopped bullets that should have killed her. "If I'd gotten a good look at any of them, you'd have had bodies left behind," she said angrily.

"You did your best," the Executioner said, his voice softening, becoming gently soothing. "I've been to the scene, and the signs were there that you were outgunned Two dead and four wounded was a far better result than all of you dying. And you saved the noncombatants, buying them time to escape."

Walters sighed. Her brow furrowed as she digested his words. Bolan hoped that his short speech planted a few seeds of comfort. "Did you check on Colonel Storm?" she asked.

"He'll recover," Spelling answered. "He's still in intensive care, but his condition is improving."

Walters managed a weak smile.

"Did you see which way the helicopters turned?" Bolan inquired. The question was soft, as if he didn't want his voice to bruise her wounded form.

Walters swallowed, then nodded. "They turned northwest," she stated. "About thirty degrees off straight north."

Spelling's face showed skepticism. "That's a pretty exact estimate."

Bolan glared at his partner.

"I'm a soldier first. That means I know how to do three things—shoot a rifle, plan a patrol with a map and follow that patrol without help. I'm not saying their exact course, but…" Walters paused, coughing.

Bolan rested his hand on her shoulder. "Just relax. Okay?"

"One of the scientists…he was a veteran," Walters whispered, her voice rough from the pain. "He pitched in on the final defense. They killed him, and they killed Crystal, and left the rest of us as wreckage."

Bolan nodded. He'd known the scientist, if only briefly,

as an ally. The loss of a comrade in arms, one he'd actually met, weighed on his shoulders heavily.

"Just make sure they pay," Walters said.

"I will," Bolan answered her. "They won't get away with this."

CARSON KELLY LOOKED at the man who stood at the gates of the compound, a knapsack slung over his shoulder. He knew the nondescript person as a skilled, deadly warrior who had managed to recruit the Militia of Truth and Justice away from a psychopathic millionaire who sought to hold the nation hostage. Kelly's guards watched him warily, as he'd appeared out of the forest like a ghost rising from the mist.

"Carson," Richards greeted him.

"You took a chance approaching this facility," Kelly replied.

Richards nodded. "I feel that the risk is worth it."

Kelly motioned for the man in the guardhouse to retract the chain-link gate on silent, electrically powered motors and hydraulic runners. Richards set down his sack and walked forward, empty-handed in greeting. Kelly took the offered hand.

"What kind of risk?" Kelly asked.

Richards looked at the M-16 wielding guards surrounding him. "The world as we know it is about to come to an end."

Kelly raised an eyebrow. "How so?"

"I have discovered a conspiracy within the government that has been slowly guiding the world toward a flash point," Richards stated. "This same conspiracy had me under drug therapy, trying to turn me into their mindless puppet."

Kelly nodded. "Walk with me. At ease, men."

Richards walked back and shouldered his knapsack after

a sentry finished examining it with a scanner wand. The sentry noted the handguns and spare magazines within, telling Kelly of their presence.

"This is a warrior. To ask him to go unarmed is folly," Kelly said. "He left his weapons in his bag as a show of respect. If he'd wanted, our security perimeter wouldn't have slowed him down."

The guards looked at Richards.

"This is the truest example of our ideal," Kelly continued. "He has fought against corruption and tyranny across the world. I have seen him walk through the fires of hell, and he has entered this compound before, not as a friend, but he has since earned that appellation."

Richards kept his face impassive, fighting against his embarrassment for a moment. His history with the MTJ leader had a few healed-over scars, but it was the basis of a trusting friendship. The two hundred members of the MTJ would be a vital ally on Richards's side.

"What is it?" Kelly asked as they walked toward his office.

"We're going to take out the cancer in Washington, D.C.," Richards stated. "I've acquired some transports and have an elite fighting force, but a handful of men won't be enough."

"You have my entire army at your command," Kelly replied.

"Thank you, Carson," Richards said. "I'll need every one of them. This is going to be a blow struck for truth and justice, just as you've always wanted. We'll be going up against an enemy that has been burrowing into the heart of our society, poisoning our ideals."

"We've been aware of this presence," Kelly said. "I was just wondering when you'd get around to them."

"They had me on a chemical leash, feeding their lies into my ideals," Richards replied. "It took the efforts of a brave man to free me from their hold. But now, I fear the hounds of hell are going to be hot on our heels. They've branded me a dangerous terrorist."

"We've been considered such as well," Kelly admitted. "What is one more slur against our name? In the end, we'll have made our statement of freedom. I would rather be a martyr than a sheep under tyranny."

"Bless you, my brother," Richards said, giving Kelly a strong handshake. "We will have a chance. And if my plan comes off correctly, we'll wake up to a new world, where corruption and terror are on the run."

"Oh?" Kelly asked.

"One of my plans is to seal the southern border, and to make Asia an inhospitable wasteland," Richards stated. "It will give the world pause, keeping them away from our gates when they have other crisis points to deal with. Your men will be a vital part of obtaining the arsenal that will not only purge our government of corruption, but destroy our enemies."

Kelly's eyes widened. "Nuclear weapons?"

Richards shook his head as they finished their trek to Kelly's office. "I want the world to stand a chance. Nukes would make things impossible for life after the apocalypse we unleash. We're talking about some serious extinction weaponry."

"Biologicals?" Kelly asked.

"Biologicals. Chemicals. Directed radiation," Richards rattled off. "That way China won't be able to retaliate against us. They'll be too busy reenacting *28 Days Later.*"

Kelly swallowed. "How are you sure it won't come back here?"

"The Pacific Ocean. The weapon renders anything more complicated than animalistic behavior impossible. They won't have the capacity to board airplanes. China will rip itself apart, and knowing Beijing, they'll be firebombing and nuking their own territory to stop the plague," Richards said.

Kelly let out a long, low whistle. "But the border?"

"A different idea," Richards answered. "I'd explain more, but you'd think I was mad."

Kelly nodded. "And the government?"

Richards smirked. "Well, I did exaggerate the fact that we won't be using nuclear weapons. Especially since most of our enemies are tucked tightly into very specific pockets that aren't necessary to feed the nation. We lose two, three coastal cities at the most."

Kelly chuckled. "I love your mind."

Richards nodded. "Come on, we have to get the men ready to travel to Maryland. My partners will have your weapons and other equipment ready by the time we get there."

7

The helicopter sliced through the skies toward the Idaho border, following the course that had been indicated by Sergeant Emily Walters only hours earlier. Mack Bolan and Winslow Spelling sat next to each other in the back as Jack Grimaldi kept the breakneck pace in the cockpit.

"Thirty degrees northwest from the XH-92 hangar, within a few hours travel by helicopter," Bolan said. He made a circle in erasable marker on an acetone map. He looked to Spelling.

"In this particular area—" Spelling pointed to the map, using a different colored marker "—this is the location of an armed organization called the Militia of Truth and Justice. Heard of them?"

Bolan nodded. "I just hadn't gotten around to them yet. They'd popped up on my radar recently, but apparently the Justice Department got word that they were neutralized."

"In a way, they were," Spelling replied. "Cameron encountered a conspiracy that had utilized them as pawns. However, even under the drugs, he did have a sort of ethical core."

"Ethical core?" Bolan asked. "He shoots unarmed women in the face."

"I said a sort," Spelling stated. "To Cameron, the men

in this militia were guilty of loving their country too much. He couldn't bear to punish them for their patriotism."

Bolan swallowed hard. "If the MTJ loved their country, they wouldn't murder their fellow citizens."

"Cameron saw it differently. Yours is not the only point of view," Spelling stated. "The conspiracy fell because of that organization."

Bolan's eyes narrowed. "If you're trying to gain sympathy for your cousin…"

"I'm not," Spelling explained. "I'm just explaining how he thinks."

The Executioner spoke into his boom mike. "Jack, we're getting close. Any aerial activity?"

"I've got traces on radar," Grimaldi replied. "It could be the competition moving in."

"Drop us off here," Bolan said. "We'll hoof it the rest of the way while you run silent and deep. If we need help, then you can become noise and thunder."

"Got it," Grimaldi answered.

"Lock and load, Spelling," Bolan ordered. "Time to begin earning your keep."

EZEKIEL CUTTER and Raymond Jance could both tell that their duty, to stay behind in the Militia of Truth and Justice's base, was not going to be a simple case of losing out on some action. They, and the squad of soldiers under their command, could feel it in the air after the rest of the homegrown army left to make the trek to the East Coast. They could sense the tension in the air, the held breath of brutal violence ready to explode.

With their rifles cocked, locked and ready, and an assortment of Claymore mines set around the camp, Cutter and Jance would unleash hell on anyone Richards felt was on his tail.

"It will be a glorious battle," Cutter said, his voice wistful.

"Keep your mind about your business," Jance admonished. "We are trusted to delay and disorganize the opposition. Dying prematurely will hinder the plans of our allies."

Cutter grinned. "I will not sacrifice my life foolishly."

"Excellent," Jance returned. "The wind sounds strange this dawn. As if—"

"Stealth helicopters," Cutter cut him off. "I caught a glimpse of something against the treetops. A pilot exposed his craft for a moment, toward the south."

Jance nodded. "More than one, perhaps. That one might have exposed itself to distract us from the enemy's true avenue of approach."

Cutter put his encrypted radio to his lips. "Sniper 3 and Sniper 8, maintain watch on our southern approach. All others, maintain the rest of the loop. Anyone sees anything, open fire and call down the Claymore charges. This will be a day when we achieve recompense for Ruby Ridge and Waco!"

TO AARON KURTZMAN, an impartial, intelligent observer on the radio frequencies used by the Militia of Truth and Justice, Cutter's call to battle proved to be ironic hyperbole in at least one corner. The MTJ believed that the corrupt U.S. government had been chafing at its leash to strike at the militia. Unfortunately, in this case, they were correct. While he hadn't broken the encryption on the Rose Initiative's communications, he was able to pick up short bursts of controlled radio traffic. A squad of heavily armed commandos, split into at least two teams who maintained strict communication discipline, was descending on the back-woods paranoids with equipment that rivaled the best that Stony Man Farm could acquire.

In the other corner was Mack Bolan, paired with a member of the Rose Initiative who had switched sides to preserve his life. Bolan and Spelling had killed their radios, isolating themselves, and preventing any high-tech sur-veillance, akin to Kurtzman's, to detect their ground presence. Kurtzman figured the enemy had spotted Grimaldi's helicopter, since the MTJ's commander had sighted it. Bolan's only advantage was that the Rose Ini-tiative's troopers and the militiamen didn't know who they were facing, or how many.

That, plus the Executioner's audacious brand of all-out conflict, might carry the day for Bolan and Spelling. And if it didn't, Hal Brognola was already organizing a response to any action Richards took in Washington.

Kurtzman kept a bead on the two active radios of the Ini-tiative's commandos, tracking them through their en-crypted transmissions, but even then, he didn't have a solid lead on the numbers. The woods were cool in the Idaho fall morning, but like Bolan and Spelling, the enemy forces were wearing insulated battle suits, lowering their thermal profile, making infrared tracking by satellite difficult while the tree canopy made even the supersensitive cameras of the NRO satellites all but useless.

The Executioner was on his own, against two enemy forces. One was an entrenched, paranoid militia with a ring of snipers and antipersonnel mines. The other was a high-tech commando unit of unknown numbers, but sig-nificant weaponry.

Kurtzman took a sip of coffee, offering a silent prayer

for the big warrior. The infrared satellite picked up a muzzle-flash, and the battle began in earnest.

"What have you got?" Cutter barked over the radio as Kurtzman listened in.

"Men in camouflage. They have a low infrared profile, but they forgot about a rifleman behind every blade of grass," answered one of the perimeter snipers. He was whispering, but breathless, as if he were crawling in a quick scurry through the brush. "Body armor because the one I hit went down, but was still moving."

"Claymores?" Cutter asked.

"Keep them in reserve," the sniper answered. He sounded as if he were settling into his new hide.

"I hope you're getting this, Striker," Kurtzman whispered.

"Doubtful," Hunt Wethers spoke up. "That was a suppressed weapon, judging by the low muzzle-flash."

"Firing a supersonic bullet in a heavy forest. The sonic boom as the bullet passed trees would be obvious," Kurtzman countered.

"That's right," Wethers replied. "Then he should have an idea where the opening shot was."

"New firefight beginning," Carmen Delahunt announced, putting the image up on the main screen.

Hell was officially in session.

THE EXECUTIONER HEARD the solitary shot, but the crackle as the high-velocity rifle bullet snapped past tree trunks, compressed air popping against their barks, made anything more precise than a rough estimate of the location impossible. His choice for the raid on the MTJ was a full-length M-16/M-203 with a low-power Aimpoint red-dot scope.

Spelling also felt unhindered by the full-length

M-16/M-203 as he moved quickly and quietly behind the Executioner. "The fun's starting," he whispered.

Bolan glanced back at the turncoat. "Good. Let them even the odds. Noise discipline."

Spelling nodded.

In the distance, a pair of rifles opened up, silenced bullets ripping from a concealed position, their rapid passage through the forest releasing crackling lines of pops. Bolan concealed himself to one side of a trunk, scanning for the potential target. He spotted a trio of camouflage-clad commandos scurrying to cover. Spelling was crouched by a tree a yard away from Bolan, then snapped his fingers, pointing down.

Bolan knew what the operative was showing him. It was the reason he hadn't chosen that tree for cover. In the gnarled roots, covered by leaves, a radio-controlled Claymore mine was nestled. The Executioner's keen eyes had picked it up immediately, and went to a tree whose roots were bare of ground clutter where a directional antipersonnel mine could be placed. He gave Spelling a nod, then motioned for him to find other cover.

The MTJ base was a death trap, encircled with high-tech mines and barbed wire, as well as dedicated riflemen. Only the fact that the commandos were wearing quality body armor had bought the conspirators time to retreat. Bolan picked up a rock and threw it at a commando who thought he'd found cover. The man was startled enough that he yelped and stepped into the open. The MTJ snipers poured rounds into the shocked gunman, the salvo of rifle bullets defeating his body armor by sheer volume. Another Rose Initiative soldier opened fire with the grenade launcher under his rifle, a 40 mm shell turning one of the sniper hides into a churning caldron of dismembered limbs and mangled weapons.

Spelling ripped off a burst, decapitating the grenadier swiftly before he could realize that he'd been flanked. Unfortunately, Bolan's reluctant ally drew the attention of the remaining sniper. Automatic fire chopped against the trunk Spelling was concealed behind. The Executioner whipped around and launched his own M-203 grenade, the antipersonnel bomb sinking into the ground just behind the subdued muzzle-flash of the sniper's silenced rifle. An instant later, smoke vomited out of the sniper's nest, as carnage erupted in the middle of the forest.

"Thanks for the save," Spelling whispered.

Bolan glared at him. "Now the enemy knows that there are two separate forces converging on them. And that we're at odds with each other."

Claymores burst in the distance, and Bolan knew that one of the enemy commando teams was suffering a lethal spray of high-velocity buckshot and shrapnel. No matter what body armor the fighters wore, the M-18 Claymore mine would wreak havoc on their number. Exposed limbs would be slashed to ribbons, and even Kevlar with trauma plates would have enough weak points to allow a deadly missile to slip in a hole and burrow into vital life processes.

Bolan motioned for Spelling to follow him, and the pair raced through the woods, toward where the multiple mines had gone off. If anything, that area was now the weak spot in the MTJ's defenses.

Apparently, the Rose Initiative commandos were under the same impression, because the Executioner picked up the presence of another trio of armed men speeding along parallel to them. Both groups ground to a halt, seeking cover behind tree trunks. The RI gunmen initiated fire, raking Spelling's position with a storm of 5.56 mm rounds. Bolan kept his attention on the MTJ compound and caught sight of movement among the militiamen.

The Executioner fired from the hip to drive the enemy snipers deeper into their cover and to hinder their marksmanship. "You're exposed!" he shouted.

Spelling took the hint, but bolts of supersonic lead continued to snap all around him, keeping him pinned. Rather than step into the open to seek cover from the compound, he reloaded his grenade launcher and fired. The high explosive antipersonnel round shook the barbed wire and chainlink fence, turning the metal battlements into ruptured, ragged shrapnel that sprayed into the compound. The tree trunk was thick enough to stop the lightweight, hypersonic M-16 rounds trying to chop Spelling's back to ribbons.

"It's only a temporary solution," Spelling called back. "Got a plan?"

Bolan didn't answer with words, but deeds. Spelling's thunderbolt had caused enough of a distraction for him to race closer to the compound's perimeter. In the mad dash, he scooped up an M-18 Claymore and curved back toward Spelling's position. Bolan paused just long enough to jam his own C-4 against the back of the Claymore, securing it with a piece of duct tape and inserting a small pencil detonator. Spelling widened his eyes at the sight of the high-explosive weapon in Bolan's hand, then watched the Executioner lob it underhanded around a tree trunk. The curved plate tumbled in the air, a clumsy missile that hit the dirt and skidded before coming to a halt.

The pencil detonator finished its burn-through and set

off the plastic explosives. A sympathetic detonation in the core of the mine vomited a wave of seven hundred steel ball bearings into the air. A Rose Initiative gunner who saw the curved plate land at his feet was right on top of the mine as it went off. The high-velocity shrapnel turned him to human puree.

Ricocheting shrapnel, bouncing off the hard objects Bolan's victim carried, or off nearby tree trunks, scored stunning injuries on the remaining two gunmen in the RI squad. One of them stumbled into the open, and Spelling took the opportunity to rip off a quick burst in revenge for their murder attempt on him. The 72-grain hollowpoint rounds sliced through Kevlar in the man's vest, but the majority of Spelling's rounds plunked and decelerated violently against the armor's ceramic trauma plates. Unfortunately, the trauma plates didn't cover the commando's whole torso, and the powerful rounds slipped clean through the Kevlar and into vital organs.

Bolan took out the last of the gunmen, firing a single shot through the nasal cavity of the commando. The trooper's nose disintegrated as the Executioner's bullet tore through skin and cartilage.

"Six down," Spelling said. "At least out here."

"Don't count the dead until it's over," Bolan growled. "Pull away from the perimeter, now!"

Spelling didn't have to be told twice as he broke into a run. MTJ snipers cut loose through the ruptured fence, and two Claymore mines detonated.

Bolan wove through the trees, the high-velocity shrapnel stopped by the thick trunks. The MTJ had blown their wad in this section of the compound, and he skidded to a halt. Spelling linked back up to him.

"They have snipers covering the hole we made," Spelling said.

"But this far out, they don't have a clear shot at us," Bolan replied. "We cut through the middle back to our old position, then soften the edges a little more."

"Anyone ever tell you you're crazy?" Spelling asked.

"Not in the last five minutes," Bolan answered.

The Executioner started back toward the compound, keeping an eye out for more Rose Initiative gunmen. He didn't see any, but that didn't mean he was going to slow down and make himself an easier target. Spelling was hot on his heels, and the two men slid behind an uneven berm of packed earth. Rifle rounds snapped through the forest over their heads, from the compound, but someone else on their flank opened fire as well. Bolan, however, was prepared for that eventuality, their current position protected on either side by thick trees.

"Both sides sound like they're focusing on us first," Spelling noted.

Bolan sighted the compound with his grenade launcher and sailed a 40 mm round through the torn fence. A camouflage netting tent erupted, Bolan's incendiary shell turning the nylon into a flaming blossom that disgorged smoke. Bolan slipped on a pair of goggles to protect his vision, pulling a scarf up over his nose and mouth to filter out the choking cloud created by his incendiary round.

With an inferno suddenly ablaze in their midst, the MTJ gunmen were distracted. Billowing clouds spread out through the gap created by Spelling earlier, pouring out over the pair.

"Move in," Bolan ordered.

They charged into the churning cloud, slipping among

the Militia of Truth and Justice. The pair had finally breached the compound, but they still had the militia on one side and more commandos at their back.

The Executioner didn't mind. He'd reengineered the cross fire between the two groups. The chaos and confusion were his protective cloak, enabling him to continue his mission of cleansing fire.

8

Winslow Spelling was hot on Mack Bolan's heels as the pair tore into the Militia of Truth and Justice's armed compound. The hard site was operating on a skeleton crew. Bolan's quarry, the elusive Cameron Richards, had recruited the militia for an operation against the Rose Initiative, the United States government, and enemies perceived and real of Richards's ideal America. The fact that he was going up against other commandos sent by the Rose Initiative, an organization he had been part of only hours before, was unsettling, but Spelling knew that he was damaged goods in the eyes of the ruthless covert operations organization.

The moment he'd been captured, Spelling's death sentence had been passed by the Rose Initiative, and no amount of finagling would get him back in their good graces. Right now, it was kill or be killed, and with the M-16/M-203 in his grasp, Spelling was damn well certain to unleash as much kill as he could before he went down.

A MTJ member opened fire from Spelling's right flank, and he whirled, triggering a salvo of 5.56 mm rounds. His new commander moved too swiftly, making Spelling the more attractive target for the militia snipers, but the operative didn't bear any malice toward his only ally in the shadow war he found himself fighting. The man was treating him as an equal partner in this hunt, and at least

he gave Spelling the chance to fight back and live as long
as he could. Spelling's burst of autofire tore into the militiaman, a half-dozen rounds shredding through flesh and
bone. The sniper gurgled as he collapsed into a heap of
useless limbs.

Spelling almost counted another one down, but then he
remembered the big man's admonition of not tallying the
score until the battle was over. Sure enough, the crackle of
more rifle fire ripped through the air, and Spelling ducked
against the side of a cabin. Bullets splintered the rough
wooden planks making up the structure, rounds chewing
through, but not enough to strike the operative.

Stopping on a dime, the Executioner ground to a halt,
swung around and opened fire with his own M-16, tapping
out a short burst. Spelling glanced around the corner and
spotted Bolan's target, a Rose Initiative commando, most of
his face erased by a blast of high-velocity rifle rounds. Bolan
was up and moving, as if he hadn't skipped a beat. Spelling
stayed on the Executioner's heels, realizing that working
with him was his sole chance at escaping the pit he'd found
himself in. The man had a brain like a combat computer, and
his reflexes were honed to match that lightning quick mind.

"A way out," Spelling whispered. Hope surged, giving
Spelling's feet the wings they needed to keep up with the
solitary warrior.

JANCE SNARLED IN RAGE as he pulled the tarp off the RPD
light machine gun. He swung it toward the center of the
camp. Smoke was billowing everywhere thanks to the incendiary grenade launched into it. He held down the
trigger, and 7.62 mm thunderbolts spit from the Russian
weapon's long barrel. The high-powered rounds snapped

and cracked, even though he had nothing to aim at in the obfuscating swirls of smoke choking the camp.

"Stop wasting ammo!" Cutter snapped. "We still have a team outside the perimeter!"

Cutter punctuated his point by firing a round through his Winchester Model 70. The hunting rifle spiked a bullet into the body armor of a Rose Initiative commando and hurled the gunman into a lifeless heap. A single 7 mm Remington Magnum round, meant to humanely kill large mule deer during hunting season, also proved a ballistic juggernaut on the battlefield. Cutter threw the bolt on his rifle and fed another soft-point bullet into the chamber. He sighted on a commando and triggered the rifle.

The man's polycarbonate face shield disintegrated, deforming the lead-cored, copper-jacketed bullet as it did so. When the 7 mm round finally contacted the trooper's face, it was a whirling fan of flattened metallic petals, spinning sideways, drilling through flesh and bone.

Two enemy corpses down, Cutter thought. That still didn't make the odds even. The south perimeter had taken a brutal hammering, and the eastern fence was completely breached. For all Cutter knew, the armored commandos were pouring in by the platoon through the shattered fence.

"Movement!" Jance shouted. He swung the RPD, and the light machine gun rattled off its death song, a quarter of a drum of ammunition popping out the muzzle like the sputtering of a vengeful hell beast.

Cutter's instincts kicked in and he rolled away from Jance, clutching his rifle tightly to his chest. An instant later, the MTJ machine gunner disappeared in a blossom of shredded flesh and concussive waves. Jance's mangled RPD machine gun jutted barrel-first from the ground thirty yards away.

Cutter grimaced, cursing the loss of Jance, but the man had drawn too much attention with his flaring muzzle-flash. The men who had gotten into the compound had to have had grenade launchers, and had the skill and will to utilize them with impunity. He crawled along, keeping under the thick smoke that hovered like a cloak. He could breathe easier on the ground, and he spotted the enemy's feet.

He swung his rifle around and aimed into the cloud. The shot broke too quickly, and Cutter sizzled a 7 mm mangler to the right of one pair of feet. The two men split up, charging for cover in the camp.

Without a good solid target, Cutter knew that staying still was tantamount to suicide. He moved quickly, crawling into a rut and scurrying along the bottom. All around, the sounds of the three-way combat rattled, every so often a scream of dying horror punctuating a lessening of the odds for one group or another.

Unfortunately, Cutter mused, the three-way fight seemed not to have taken its toll on the third party, the ones who'd gutted the MTJ compound and now danced in its smoldering entrails. He plucked a grenade off his harness and looked out at the cushion of air between the cloud and the ground. He saw a pair of legs and hurled his grenade toward it. The militiamen wouldn't be moving in the center of the camp, so it had to be the intruders.

The arming lever popped loose from the minibomb with the sound of a plucked spring, 6.5 ounces of high explosive wrapped in lethal metal shrapnel sailing toward its target.

MACK BOLAN HEARD the distinctive metallic *clink* of a grenade spoon as it popped loose from its warhead. He looked through the swirling smoke. He was caught in the open, equally distant from his two closest places of cover. Bolan's weight was settling on his right foot, and he whipped his head around, pushing the words out.

"Grenade! Cover!" Bolan roared to Spelling.

His muscles in his right leg tensed, coiling up for his next step, and he knew that he had to make a choice. The spoon release meant that he had under five seconds to pick a place to dive for cover, and he'd already burned off a second and a half warning Spelling and getting his body aligned to dive. In the meantime, his lifetime of experience in battlefields was being pushed into fast forward as he sought a possible avenue of escape. He knew how the enemy had spotted him, and for a flickering hundredth of a second, his eyes snapped down to his feet.

The grenadier had spotted Bolan because the smoke wasn't all encompassing. There was a cushion of air close to the ground, clear for breathing. From the thighs up, Bolan was an invisible phantom, but to an opponent crouched under that, he was clearly visible.

The Executioner's legs snapped straight, the powerful muscles of his thighs and calves launching him into the cloud completely. Airborne, he knifed through the concealing smoke, and he saw the shadow of his next point of cover loom into view. The pickup truck would provide good protection against the shrapnel of the fragmentation grenade. Bolan reached a hand out and grabbed the lip of the pickup's bed, arm muscles protesting as they fought to alter his momentum.

Bolan's grasp was up to the task, and he dumped himself in the protective tub of metal and fiberglass lining the pickup's bed just as the fragger split the smoke with its thunderclap. The concussion wave rushed over the open lip, and Bolan pulled his hand down under cover, even as a notch of razor wire sliced across his knuckle. Had the Executioner been a heartbeat slower, he'd have been riddled with high-velocity fragments of shattered metal wire and casing fragments. No amount of body armor would have been able to protect him from the close-range exposure to the lethal metal radiating out from the fiery blast core of the grenade detonation.

Bolan lay in the back of the truck, looking through the smoke, now completely invisible to his opponent, but also knowing that he couldn't see anything of the grenadier. He was tempted to respond with a 40 mm hell bomb of his own, but stayed his hand. He wanted information, and despite the forensic scientists that Brognola already had working on this case, live men told tales faster than dead ones. He looked over the edge of the truck bed and spotted the smeared silhouette of Spelling tucked against a corner, making a hand movement. Spelling wanted to use his grenade launcher to reduce their opponent to jelly.

Bolan held up his hand in the signal for stop. Spelling obeyed, and the Executioner was heartened by Spelling's acceptance of his authority. He reached into his thigh pouch and ran his bare fingertips over the Braille lettering on the trio of canister grenades. The Braille labels were included so that operators could tell their combat warload apart in the dark or when blinded by smoke. Bolan plucked a Def-Tec distraction device from the pouch, popped the pin and hurled it toward the grenade launch site.

The blinding effects of the distraction device wouldn't be permanent, but the Executioner jumped down and charged a downed militiaman at full speed. The man thrashed, heels kicking into the dirt. Bolan gave him a temporary peace from his pain, knocking him out with a hard cuff to the jaw with the butt of his rifle. Out cold, the MTJ man would be a source of valuable intel.

Spelling finally caught up with Bolan.

"Secure the prisoner. I'll finish cleaning house," the Executioner explained. "Don't let this one die. I'm not going to waste time taking any more prisoners."

Spelling nodded. No arguments were coming from the ex-Rose Initiative operator. Maybe it'd taken the first hard contact with his former comrades to shake Spelling's cockiness loose.

However it came about, Bolan was glad for the change in attitude. Spelling deftly bound the prisoner's wrists and ankles with cable ties, and when he finished, crouched, ready to defend the tightened perimeter around the prisoner. Bolan went from watching Spelling's back to doing what he did best.

Bringing hell to the enemy.

It was made easier as a pair of Militia of Truth and Justice gunmen raced around a corner, hoping to come to the aid of their fellow fighters. Instead of dispensing their racist form of justice, they received the blazing heat of a trio of 5.56 mm NATO rounds burning through each of their entrails. The MTJ shooters were beaten to the draw by the Executioner, and they fell under his barrage.

Another militiaman staggered through the smoke, unable to tell who was friend or foe because he had no eye protection and the stinging cloud ravaged his tear ducts. Bolan was unhindered, thanks to his own preparations. He pivoted the M-16 and punched a single bullet through the gunman's open mouth before he could tell that the Executioner was a foe. The militiaman toppled to the ground.

Bolan turned in the direction the gunner had come from, reloading his rifle on the move. His hands operated with practiced precision, independent of his eyes and feet, which were busy navigating him through the choking maze of the burning compound. Ammunition began to cook off in one corner of the camp, bullets cracking as the fire spread to the militia's armory. Bolan leveled his M-203 at the source of the gunfire and triggered a high-explosive shell. The thunderbolt lanced into the slowly building conflagration and snuffed it out with the authority of several ounces of TNT. The power-load flattened the arsenal, blew out the flames and created a firebreak.

"Fuck you!" a choked voice gurgled.

Bolan sidestepped, putting a corner between himself and the opponent, a well-honed reflex action that saved his life once again as a stream of AK-47 slugs ripped through the air. Half-blinded by the smoke, the militia rifleman had almost gotten the drop on the Executioner. Unfortunately for him, a person got only one free shot at Mack Bolan. The MTJ man tried to press his attack, staggering closer, firing a second burst at Bolan's cover, but the Executioner dropped to the ground, rolled out from behind the corner and emptied a short burst into the shooter. Rifle rounds stitched the determined militiaman up the center, killing him instantly.

Bolan got to his feet and circled around toward Spelling's position, keeping an eye out for more activity within the compound's fence. Outside, the Rose Initiative would be another thorny proposition for him, but with the MTJ cleared and secured, he would tackle that task more easily.

Bolan could see a sprawled corpse collapsed in the dirt. The dead man wore the commando armor of one of the

Rose Initiative. The Executioner took cover, not wanting to pop up on his reluctant partner when he was in the middle of a defensive action. They were operating under radio silence to avoid tipping off the enemy to their tactics and position.

A pair of commandos were moving in on Spelling's flank, and Bolan took them down with a slash of high-velocity rounds that mowed them down like a scythe through a field of grain. Spelling turned, glanced at the dead pair, then threw a thumbs-up to let Bolan know that he was aware of the help.

Spelling sent a hand signal to Bolan to keep moving. The Executioner knew the logic of the plan. Since Spelling was no doubt the focus of the enemy's activity as a hemmed-in target, he'd make a good anvil for Bolan to be the hammer. The Rose Initiative gunmen caught in the middle would be crushed by their coordinated actions.

Bolan began his orbit of Spelling's position, hunting through the thinning smoke for other foes. He knew that he'd also provide a good distraction, taking the heat off Spelling and their prisoner.

Bolan didn't want to lose their captive to the Initiative. The man had a few choice words to spill before the Executioner would let him escape his judgment.

The Rose Initiative commandos had only one avenue of entry into the compound, and that was through the hole that Bolan and Spelling had blasted only moments before. The Executioner sighted a quartet of the gunners who remained at the perimeter breach, acting as rear security for their advance teams. Their rifles chattered, spraying at Bolan as he caught their attention with a quick dash across open ground. The riflemen were too late to hit the warrior.

Countless battles had educated Bolan about exactly how much reaction time was needed to see a target and fire at it. He'd chosen a stretch of ground to provide him just enough space to draw the enemy's attention. One of them was on his communicator, and Bolan heard the sudden rattle of rifle fire from a different flank.

The soldiers were communicating, working together in trying to hem in the Executioner. Instead, they betrayed the location of one of their fire teams As soon as the rifles opened up, Spelling fired a 40 mm shell into the midst of the gunners. Shrapnel and high explosives reduced the shooters to shredded remains.

Spelling's explosive elimination of the fire team spurred activity from two more, their weapons chattering impotently at the frame of an old tractor, its big steel wheels providing their former comrade and his prisoner with considerable protection. Bolan popped up and targeted the closest fire team. He drew his suppressed Beretta to make this kill, hoping to maximize the element of surprise. His first shot was a 9 mm pill through the cheekbone of one armored rifleman. The dying man jerked violently, jostling his partner.

The rifleman turned his head, looking at what the problem was, when he found himself the recipient of another dose of death from the Executioner's Beretta. This shot clipped the underside of the commando's chin and tunneled into his throat, coming to a violent stop against the heavy bone of his spinal column. Choking on his own blood, but paralyzed by the trauma to his spinal cord, the dying trooper slumped to the ground.

Bolan grimaced and drew his Desert Eagle. He was a warrior, and not one who believed in the suffering of others. The tungsten-cored .44 Magnum round Bolan had on hand was more than sufficient to smash through the anguished soldier's helmet to provide instant relief. Unfortunately, it also exposed the Executioner to the other fire team.

Bolan didn't regret his Sergeant Mercy side, and simply shifted his aim toward the reacting riflemen as they noticed the elimination of their partners. The Desert Eagle launched two more of its hard-pointed, tungsten-cored eggs toward a gunman raising his automatic rifle. The trauma plates of his Kevlar armor shattered on contact with the heavyweight metal, ballistic nylon parting under its thunderous passage.

The second rifleman opened fire, and Bolan winced as he was a moment too slow in ducking, his shoulder carved by a hypersonic rifle bullet that tore his own protective armor. The Executioner's Beretta peppered the gunner with 9 mm rounds, but helmet and armor protected the gunman from any harm more serious than a bruise—at least from Bolan's head-on attack.

Spelling took advantage of Bolan's distraction to line up his M-16 on the second gunman and open fire. He worked the M-16 on single-shot, but his training was such that he still fired off five rounds so quickly it sounded like one. It was standard military training, a faster, more controlled means of engaging an enemy target, as long as the sights and a strong stance was utilized. Two of Spelling's bullets were stopped by the commando's armor, but the other three tore through areas where there was only Kevlar covering the man's vital organs. Spelling turned from the dropped rifleman and glanced to Bolan's position.

The Executioner rose enough to give his partner a hand signal. The enemy was in motion, and it was time to finish it. Spelling turned his attention to the perimeter breach and saw that the quartet was abandoning its post to wade into battle.

Bolan softened them up with a 40 mm grenade that struck one of their number in the abdomen. The plastic explosive ripped his body in two and flattened the others to the ground. Spelling fired, pumping out his 5-round strings of rapid fire, riddling the fallen gunmen, regardless of whether they were stunned or dead.

It was ruthless, Bolan thought, but it was also practical. They couldn't waste any more time. For all the gunfire in the MTJ compound, there were still two enemy helicopters in the area. Grimaldi was orbiting the hard site, but Bolan didn't want to expose his pilot unnecessarily.

Bolan keyed him in on the radio.

"The other birds took off," Grimaldi said. "They obviously had orders to withdraw. We're alone."

"There's a spot by the motor pool large enough to land," Bolan said. "We've got a prisoner."

Bolan looked at Spelling, who dragged the unconscious and bound captive by his ankles. "Seems like I left the prisoner in good hands."

Grimaldi sounded doubtful as he made his next pronouncement. "That's good news."

9

Hal Brognola listened as Bolan and Spelling reported the results of their interrogation of Cutter, the Militia of Truth and Justice lieutenant that they had captured. What they had to say wasn't pretty.

"Cameron Richards has a crew of sympathetic agents on his side and has recruited a violent and well-trained white supremacist militia called the Militia of Truth and Justice," Bolan stated.

"Richards was the Rose Initiative's chief enforcement arm. He was the one man to call when everything else failed, but he's broken his leash. The Initiative is trying to rein him in, but there is no indication that they have a better lead on Richards than we do," Spelling said.

"As far as we can tell, the Initiative was started in the very late sixties or early seventies. They seemed to have official sanction at first, but they slowly slipped their ties once the reorganization caused by the scandals of the Nixon administration started becoming apparent," Brognola stated. "They still operated in the U.S. government's best interests, but they covered their tracks well enough that they were forgotten.

"Ironically, we've been providing a shadow for the Rose Initiative to do its work," Bolan said.

The big fed winced. "A group that doesn't exist, operating in the shadow of another group that doesn't exist.

Rumors of their existence would end up attributed to you. I've had Bear going over the backlog of urban legends and rumors of activities that could have belonged to us to see if they might be Richards. We got some stories from Dozier. Bear's vetting some things, but discovering a pattern for our enemy."

"Richards has an army of approximately two hundred men. Richards and the MTJ have gone completely off the radar and are laying low, utilizing drug-smuggling pipelines and other modes of off-grid transportation," Bolan said.

"Off-grid?" Brognola asked.

"Buses, boxcars and hitchhiking. Approximately two hundred men, unarmed and indistinguishable from any other U.S. citizen, are drifting from Idaho to Maryland. They will assemble somewhere, and knowing Richards as much as we do, it will be in a facility that the regular agencies have no eyes on. Richards's known associates, Henry Costell and Jacob Weist, were sent ahead to assemble an arsenal and a staging area for an assault on Washington, D.C., to get into something known only as the Arsenal," the Executioner said.

Brognola looked at the files. "Martial law might stop some of them, but we'd still have a trained commando unit with stealth helicopters and a ton of weaponry ready to move on Washington. We have the resources of multiple law-enforcement agencies at our fingertips, and we're doing our best to track down members of the MTJ as they're migrating to the coast. Outstanding arrest warrants are being circulated to state and local agencies."

"Even so, that leaves the Rose Initiative, and this Arsenal," Bolan said.

"The Initiative has acquired a variety of dangerous

weapons over its decades of service to the nation," Spelling said.

"Nuclear missiles?" Brognola asked.

"Among other things," Bolan stated. "We're looking at three decades of prototypes for weapons we're seeing in development now. Technology-destroying electromagnetic pulse weapons, mood altering ultra-low sonic frequency generators and bio-plagues that concentrate on crops and livestock indigenous to certain regions, to name a few.

"There are a half-dozen scientifically plausible scenarios that Spelling suggests, and a dozen that sound crazy, but that Spelling states are real enough," Bolan said. "And the half dozen we've run threat projections on are the stuff of nightmares."

"Can we trust him?" Brognola asked.

"The Initiative wants him dead," Bolan stated. "We don't have much choice."

Brognola grimaced. "Do what you can, Striker," he said.

AARON KURTZMAN GOT to work on the information the Executioner had extracted from his prisoner. Armed with a location, the Stony Man cybernetics genius cast out his electronic net over Baltimore. From pay phone taps to monitoring cell tower networks in the immediate vicinity of the train yard, the intelligence warriors at Stony Man Farm reached into the electronic ether, fishing for clues as to where Richards might be located.

It took ten minutes, but Kurtzman and his crew picked up the first tentative link from inside their electronic dragnet. Tracking the disposable cell phone just bought at a convenience store, within the physical area, and calling outside of the Baltimore metro area, Kurtzman picked up on their first call.

"It's another buy and trash burner," Akira Tokaido announced. "These guys are good. If we'd needed a warrant to track these down, we'd be scrambling for a week."

"We're not going for prosecution here," Kurtzman reminded his young apprentice. "We're just pointing Striker at him."

Kurtzman kept his concentration on the momentary cell phone linkage that they had. Using some of the most powerful satellites in orbit over the Eastern Seaboard, they followed the radio signals and high-speed telemetry to home in on who was receiving the call.

Carmen Delahunt had already smashed the encryption on the disposable cell phones, and neither side was using any form of add-on circuitry to enhance their security. They'd assumed that anonymity and the rules of law would provide enough of a cushion.

"The compound in Idaho was destroyed," the militia-man said. "They took down Jance and Cutter and the rest."

"Any survivors?" Richards asked.

"Me. A few others who ran."

"Disappear. We're going as planned," Richards responded.

Both phones cut out, but not before Kurtzman had a GPS lock on Richards's location.

"He's moving. Quickly," Delahunt stated. "I'm trying to calibrate the direction he's going, but toward the end of the conversation, he was turning in a circle."

Delahunt's brow furrowed, then she brought up a road map. "He was on an overpass."

"Staying in motion to keep from being tracked back to

his headquarters," Kurtzman grumbled. "Any messages from that phone?"

"No," Delahunt said. "But then, it's disposable. He'd chuck the damn thing into a roadside ditch and be out fifty bucks."

"Were these things made just to give me ulcers?" Kurtzman grumbled.

"Actually, they appear to have been vexing the Drug Enforcement Administration and local narcotics officers for years," Hunt Wethers interjected. "Naturally, such burners as they're named have slowly started to enter espionage usage for exactly the same reasons. They're completely anonymous and can disappear in a heartbeat, leaving anyone looking for them stumped."

Kurtzman shook his head in disgust. "Richards is closer to D.C. than he is to Baltimore."

"And he was driving there before he dumped the phone," Delahunt stated. "But simple tradecraft. We'll keep an eye out for him approaching Baltimore, while we know he's just changed lanes and is swinging back here."

"We assume," Tokaido stated. "There are plenty of places up and down the East Coast to hide. We just happen to be sitting in one such piece of prime real estate."

"And it all depends on what kind of friends they still have," Kurtzman added. "If anything, we need to track down this Arsenal that belongs to the Rose Initiative before Richards can make his move."

"Spelling's in the dark about it," Delahunt interjected.

"Maybe that's what's slowing Richards," Wethers mused. "He doesn't have a definite location either, so he's staged this delaying action to keep us guessing. He's building a cushion so that he can home in on his goal."

Kurtzman looked at the map of Washington, D.C. "The cold war necessitated the placement of government facilities all throughout this region. A dedicated search by the 101st Airborne would take a year to hit all the best spots. We're out of time, and we're in a race with the Rose Initiative and Richards's group."

"Why would the Initiative just sit on this Arsenal?" Tokaido asked. "Wouldn't they pack it up and move it out the minute they figured their boy was coming back down their throats?"

"That presumes sufficient transportation capability, and safeguards against containment breaches," Wethers countered. "Some stuff you just can't toss in the trunk of your shit mobile and drive off down the road."

"Leave my Gremlin out of this," Tokaido muttered. "But yeah."

"Don't forget, the defenders always have the advantage," Delahunt added. "Who knows what kind of security measures are being mobilized?"

"And considering we're dealing with trained intel operatives working off the grid, we can't track them to see where they're reporting to their boss," Kurtzman growled. "It's tempting to pull Able and Phoenix off their respective missions."

"So we have ten people sitting around, not knowing where to go?" Barbara Price inquired, walking into the Computer Room. "No. The guys have their fires to put out. We pull them, we've got other people's lives at risk."

Kurtzman nodded. "All we have over the enemy is our own brainpower."

"So, start using it. Track power usage or increased message

traffic over previously unknown lines," Price offered. "The Initiative must be mobilizing to make its stand."

"Then again, the Initiative has had several days to make their communications and upgrade their defenses," Wethers added. "So we'd have to scour four days of records, looking for power alteration patterns and transmissions. We're behind the curve."

Price shook her head. "I'll keep leaning on my CIA contacts. Maybe they'll know something about the Initiative and what forgotten facilities they might have inherited."

"Good luck with that," Kurtzman grumbled as Price turned and left the room.

THE DISPOSABLE CELL PHONE disintegrated as Richards watched it run over by a truck in the rearview mirror. No one would be able to pull data off of its ground circuit boards, so he returned his concentration to the problem at hand as Costell kept the car at a steady speed.

"They'll know we're in position," the pilot pronounced. "And if they're as good as we think they are, they might realize that we don't have our eyes on the target just yet."

"Undoubtedly," Richards returned. "But until we've narrowed down our options, we can't make a move."

"So, what do we do?" Costell asked.

"Get the information we need the old-fashioned way," Richards stated. "I'm going to look up Cornell."

"That's giving up an awful big advantage," Costell stated.

"Trading one advantage for another, my friend," Richards countered. "The Rose Initiative knows what our ultimate goal is, especially if they've been going after my competition."

"We don't even know who this enemy is," Costell noted. "They might be off the grid."

"It's a possibility," Richards stated. "Damn shame."

"What is?" Costell asked.

"That he's on their side."

Costell's brow furrowed. "The Initiative?"

"No. He's on the side of the status quo," Richards noted. "The Initiative hasn't changed its goals, it's just made us the scapegoat and wants to eliminate us. Ultimately, the Initiative is still working to make the world better for all our sakes."

"At the cost of its pawns," Costell interjected.

Richards nodded grimly.

The pair drove on.

THE SITUATION HAD BEEN upgraded from a terrorist incident in Los Angeles to a threat against the nation's capital. It was still a few hours until dawn, but Bolan wasn't going to give up while there was still a maniac on the loose.

The Executioner and his reluctant ally would continue their hunt for their opposition. The pair was back in Washington, operating out of a safehouse.

"We're running low on options," Bolan told his partner.

"And that means my ass gets wagged out in public as bait," Spelling growled.

"It's either bait, or you give me someone I can lean on," Bolan countered.

Spelling's eyes narrowed. "Colonel Martin Cornell," he said quietly.

"The man who recruited you?"

Spelling pulled a cigarette from a pack. He offered one to the Executioner, who declined the smoke. "How'd you guess?"

"All of the other names you've given came easily,"

Bolan said. "You gave up people who didn't matter much to you, but Cornell?"

"The old man gave me a reason to live. Now you're going to do what to him?" Spelling asked.

"Make him an offer he can't refuse," the Executioner said.

"He's been trained to resist interrogation," Spelling countered.

"Then you'd better appeal to his better nature fast," Bolan stated. "Because I have a feeling that Cornell might be the only handle that Richards has as well. If he had a location on the Arsenal, he wouldn't have bothered to distract us in Baltimore like that," Bolan said, not hiding his derision.

Spelling gritted his teeth. "Those men care about America. They risked their lives to maintain their cause."

"A cause of genocide," Bolan said.

Spelling looked at the Glock on the table. "You'll never understand us."

"Oh, I understand you. A bunch of blind psychopathic losers who're looking for the next scapegoat to hang their own personal failures on," Bolan answered. "Your misbegotten little crusade to cleanse America is doomed to failure, because you're not even looking at the true rot burrowing into her heart. You just see a skin color different from yours, hear a name for God different than yours, and you're ready to put a bullet through it."

"Name one thing a Muslim ever did for America," Spelling said.

"My job isn't to debate with a moron," Bolan retorted. "We have a job to do. And that means we're going to see Cornell. Now."

Spelling grumbled and stuffed his Glock into its holster,

hiding it under his jacket. "Run away from the argument like a lib—"

Bolan spun and slammed Spelling hard into the wall so hard that the defector's feet lifted from the ground. Spelling gurgled as Bolan's forearm rested against his windpipe. "Get your head out of the ground and look around. The world isn't one or the other. You're not going to get me pegged as either a liberal or a conservative. I'm my own man. I make my own decisions based on informed observations."

Bolan let Spelling collapse to the floor. The man heaved in deep breaths, looking up to the warrior before him. He spat. "You and—"

"Don't say another word, Spelling," Bolan warned. "Because if you do anything to denigrate the memory of my fellow soldiers, I'll save the Rose Initiative a lot of trouble and feed you into a wood chipper myself. I won't even waste a bullet."

"I know your type. You won't act on anger. You're too calculating," Spelling said, but doubt colored every one of his words with a nervous tremble.

"Push that button then," Bolan said. "See how much patience I have left."

Spelling swallowed his retort.

"The car. Now. You drive. We're seeing Cornell. Any deviation, and anything outside of warning me of an upcoming threat, and I'll stuff you into the glove compartment," Bolan said. He dropped the keys into Spelling's lap.

Spelling looked down at the car keys, then back up to Bolan.

"Move it."

Spelling didn't wait to be told again.

MARTIN CORNELL STUFFED the magazine into the butt of
his Beretta and snapped the slide back to chamber the top
round. He had thirteen rounds on tap, each bullet only a
hairbreadth thinner, and equally as heavy as the magnifi-
cent .45ACP that the foul little 9 mm had usurped.

The big black .40 Smith & Wesson slipped into a spare
tanker holster, augmenting his other pistols. Upon hearing
of a mass battle in Idaho, he was certain that both Cameron
Richards and the man chasing him were on their way to
deal with the Rose Initiative. Cornell had been cleaning up
and loading various handguns in supplement to his old
favored Colt 1911, and that didn't include the handguns,
shotguns and rifles of the protection detail assigned to him
by the Rose Initiative's high command.

As Richards's recruiter, he was the most publically
known face of the renegade agents. He would come to
him, knowing that he was the only one who could lead
Richards to the deadly stockpile of doomsday weaponry
accrued by the covert organization.

Cornell's lips tightened as he looked over his arms
cabinet. He reached out and picked up a Serbu special
compact shotgun. So stubby it only held four shots in its
blunt magazine and its barrel barely a foot long, the Serbu
was designed as the ultimate handgun. Capable of either
launching a .72-inch clot of lead that could tear through
flesh, bone and body armor if necessary, or spitting out a
beehive of a dozen deer-slaying buckshot rounds with a
single pull of the trigger, the Serbu was the ultimate in
close-range combat. Anyone in the same room with
Cornell would be torn in two by the killer stub gun.

Cornell figured that he would be facing armored opponents, so he opened up a box of saboted slugs, .50-caliber

rifle rounds encased in a plastic sleeve. The rifle rounds were smaller and lighter than the usual slugs used by the shotgun, but would be launched at higher velocity and had a far denser cross section, capable of rendering Kevlar and trauma plates impotent against their freight-train power.

He stuffed the Serbu into its specially designed thigh holster, folding the forward cocking lever until it was parallel to the barrel and tube magazine. Five armor-piercing rounds were in place, ready for any hard contact with a well-armed attack team. He looked at the customized M-14 on his desk, a bandolier of 20-round magazines attached to its shoulder sling.

Cornell was ready for the apocalypse to strike, and knowing Richards directly, and being told of the skills of the operative in hot pursuit of him, apocalypse wasn't an exaggeration. The two men were skilled warriors who had consistently proved their lethal abilities against superior forces, outnumbered only in bodies set against them, not out-manned in sheer ability. The two were examples of the concept of force multiplier, utilizing equal parts stealth and audacity to gain a tactical edge that nullified the defenses of heavily armed terrorist and military compounds.

Though the men in his protection detail were all veterans of brushfire wars in Africa and Indonesia, proving themselves against insurgent groups under the guise of mercenaries, rather than their true identity as deniable resources of the U.S. government, Cornell pitied the men.

They were caught between an irresistible force and an immovable object. Whatever would give in this conflict, it would be the bodyguards.

The phone warbled.

It was the head of the Rose Initiative, Hamilton Thorn.

"Come in. We can protect you better here," Thorn stated.

"No can do," Cornell replied. "My boy is out there, and we need to put him back on track. That means I'm the only one who has a chance of reaching him."

"And the other?" Thorn asked. "Given the movement patterns of both sides, we can tell that he is on the same track. He'll look for you, too. Especially since we believe he's got Spelling on his side."

Cornell sighed. "Then it's two for one. I'll bring both those kids back home, and maybe eliminate the competition."

"Are you crazy?" Thorn asked.

"I brought them both into the organization, and they've been some of our best assets," Cornell explained. "We'd be nowhere without Richards, and Spelling's been there for us too."

"Especially in Idaho where he helped gun down some of our boys," Thorn snarled.

"The boy was doing what he needed to survive," Cornell admonished. "Don't forget, you've made it no secret what will happen to our men if they were compromised. What was he supposed to do, welcome two to the head?"

Thorn snorted in disgust. "The Initiative comes first. Before our lives."

Cornell took a seat at his desk, resting his free hand on the custom-stocked M-14. The rifle had been fitted with a collapsing wire stock, which made it compact and ideal for close-quarters combat. A forward pistol grip added to its maneuverability. He preferred the M-14 to the M-16, because he never trusted the puny .22-caliber cartridge it fired. The M-14 would kick ass and take names for Cornell. "A cause without warriors to fight for it is doomed."

"Goddamned idealists," Thorn grumbled. "Just be careful."

A machine pistol's rattle was audible through the window. Cornell scooped up the M-14. "Too late for that."

10

The Executioner glanced back from the binoculars, taking note of Spelling on his six, then peered at the setup of Cornell's mansion. The estate was a couple of notches below palatial, but he wasn't hard up for room to put in a significant security force. Bolan could see a half-dozen men with rifles on the scene, and that didn't provide any indication of snipers, troops inside Cornell's house, or electronic security measures to provide a force multiplier to the bodyguard team.

"Cornell always has a dozen men on staff at his estate, but they operate in eight-hour shifts," Spelling told Bolan. "He's bulked up for the weekend, apparently."

Bolan lowered his binoculars. "You keep treating this like a party."

"You don't make jokes to ease your own tension?" Spelling inquired.

Bolan frowned. "I don't need to ease my tension."

"You're either insane, or stupid," Spelling muttered.

Bolan pocketed the binoculars, then picked up his M-16. A compact M-4 suppressor was hooked to the end of the rifle's barrel, helping to make the rifle lower profile for night combat, keeping him from making himself an easy target for enemy defenders with night vision. Spelling's rifle was similarly equipped.

"I'm focused. So should you be. Instead of burning

brainpower to come up with a quip, you should be looking for snipers," the Executioner said.

"I saw three," Spelling said, pointing out their positions.

Bolan nodded in approval. "Maybe you'd have spotted the other two instead of making up your next smart remark."

"I have a focused professional on my side," Spelling said with a sneer.

Bolan took a deep breath. "You've got it better than I do, then. Take up position here. I want you on sniper detail."

"Cornell would cut you in two if you went to him," Spelling stated. "He might come with me."

"No chance. I need sniper support," Bolan countered.

Spelling nodded. "You've stopped trusting me."

"I've got you with a rifle aimed at my back. How's that not trust?" Bolan replied. "We're still a team. We don't have to love each other, but we are working together. You put a bullet in anything aimed at me," he ordered.

Bolan slithered into the shadows.

CAMERON RICHARDS DECIDED to leave Weist and Costell with Carson Kelly and the rest of the Militia of Truth and Justice. He called in a favor from a dozen gunmen from Tennessee who called themselves the Appalachian White Coalition. They were the same disenfranchised losers that made up the Militia of Truth and Justice, just living in a different state. Rather than have Kelly think his crew was simply cannon fodder, Richards decided to use the AWC.

They were split up into four different vans, and were armed to the teeth with Heckler & Koch rifles that drifted across the border, surplus from the Colombian military. One of the vans was going to be used as a door opener. Its front grille was reinforced, and the driver was going to be inside of a tub of armor to protect him. The van was a tank, meant to draw enemy fire. It would have a ten-beat head start on the rest of the force.

Cornell's men would rain hell on that van, thinking it was an armored personnel carrier.

While the AWC kicked down the door like a rampaging rhinoceros, stirring Cornell's security like a hornet's nest, Richards planned to slip in the back door. He'd be alone, still packing a folded high-tech Heckler & Koch G-36 rifle equipped with a sound suppressor. The majority of Cornell's force would react to the blunt assault, giving Richards room to move surgically. The few bodyguards who'd form a human shield around the recruiter wouldn't be enough to protect him.

Autofire chattered in the distance. Business had begun.

Richards hooked the pole over the wall and hauled himself up. There was broken glass embedded in the top of the wall, but he slapped a Kevlar vest over the jagged, flesh-ripping shards. He used the armored pad as protection, then dropped to the other side.

Richards unhooked his jammer from his belt and plopped it on the ground. The box released pulses of radio static that left Cornell's security system blinded. With the lightning and thunder crashing in the front of Cornell's house, security would just assume that the electronic interference was coming from that angle as part of a coordinated assault. It wasn't a ruse that would last long, but it would be convincing long enough for Richards to penetrate the house and eliminate Cornell's personal bodyguards.

He spotted a shadow to his right.

Richards fired from the hip, on the run, his rifle spitting a stream of 5.56 mm slugs toward his pursuer.

BOLAN TOOK THE ONLY COVER he could, and that was a copse of slender saplings. He knew the limitations of the 5.56 mm round, and dense foliage was more than enough to turn aside the supersonic bullets. He turned his M-16 toward Richards's position and triggered his weapon, knowing that his own rounds would be slowed by the intervening cover between them. He was finally crossing fire with the rogue death dealer. The hunt from Los Angeles could have ended right then and there, but Cornell's people were more coordinated than Richards had anticipated. Rifles opened from the back of the mansion roof, sending Bolan and the death dealer diving for cover.

From his position, Spelling cut loose, a precision burst knocking a rooftop sniper out of commission. The remaining pair turned their attention to Spelling, buying both Bolan and Richards the opportunity to cut the distance to the mansion. Unfortunately for Bolan, his and Richards's courses had deviated enough that he no longer had a line on his target.

The Executioner put the stock of the M-16/M-203 to his hip and launched a 40 mm shell to the roof. He owed Spelling some assistance, and a package of high explosives bought the Rose defector some room. Shrapnel whizzed, slashing through one sniper and tearing him to pieces. The other rifleman screamed.

Bolan knew that Richards's plan had involved a full-court press through the front gates, judging by the fact that he was on his own racing through the back door. The 40 mm grenade launcher and the rifles of the rooftop snipers, however, threw a wrench into those works.

Anything that hindered Richards in his quest to unleash

Armageddon was a bonus in the Executioner's book. He still needed to get to Cornell, however.

The Rose Initiative's stockpile of doomsday weaponry had to be dismantled and neutralized. The very fact that Richards knew about, and was going after the Arsenal was a sign that even if the Initiative didn't have ulterior motives in hoarding the means of mass extinction, there were those who would be tempted by the power unleashed by such tools. How he'd eliminate the stockpile without turning the entire Eastern Seaboard into a crater, given Spelling's description of the lethal hoard, was something the Executioner would figure out when he got there.

Bolan took a running charge at one of Cornell's windows, cutting loose with the M-16, 5.56 mm rounds sparking against bullet-resistant glass. Bolan put on the brakes, preventing a clumsy collision against the pane. He keyed his throat mike, stepping to one side.

"Need a door made out of a window," he told Spelling.

"Not even a please?" Spelling griped. Despite the mocking response, Bolan heard the hollow *thunk* of the M-203. The soldier moved out of the blast radius of the high-explosive grenade. The window disappeared in a gout of smoke and debris.

"Thank you," Bolan returned.

"Ah, he does have manners," Spelling quipped. "You're welcome."

Bolan whirled, shouldering the M-16 and drawing his Desert Eagle in one swift transition. The full-length rifle would be too unwieldy in the house, while the powerful Magnum pistol was agile and accurate in Bolan's hands. Any hard contact would need the power of the .44 slugs ripping out of its six-inch barrel to make up for the lack of a full-velocity rifle round.

A security guard packing a Heckler & Koch UMP machine pistol appeared in a doorway, the weapon chattering out a quick burst trying to tag the Executioner. But Bolan's stealthy form was hard to acquire a quick target on, his shadow absorbing a churning burst of .45-caliber bullets rather than his body. The Desert Eagle snapped up and belched out a 240-grain slug that speared the Initiative gunman at the bridge of his nose. The guard crashed to the floor as two more gunners fired through the doorway.

Bolan had thrown himself behind a table just in time to protect himself from a storm of full-auto vengeance for the dead soldier. The wood splintered under the blistering assault, however, and he saw blemishes in the hardwood's underside. Bolan rolled onto his haunches, leveled the mighty .44 Magnum pistol at the part of the table where the greatest deformation was caused by enemy bullets, and cut loose right through the wood. The .45ACP slugs, moving at only half the speed of the heavier .44 rounds, didn't have much chance of cutting through the hardwood in one shot. The Desert Eagle, however, punched its rounds clean through the weakened wood, thunderbolts spearing along the firing arc of Cornell's bodyguards. One UMP fell silent as soon as the Executioner's opening salvo cut across the space between him and the shooters.

The remaining bodyguard let loose a curse, the other man screaming in shock and agony as he tried to hold coils of bubbling intestines into his bullet-ravaged belly.

"Shut up, dammit!" the bodyguard snarled.

Bolan popped up and aimed at the sound of the voice,

but the man was tucked tightly behind the wall, no shadows exposed.

Bolan aimed at the wall and cut loose, burning off the remaining five rounds in the pistol's magazine, chewing tunnels through plaster and wood before peppering the enemy gunman.

The mortally wounded gunner staggered into the open, bright blood fountaining from his lips and nose. Bolan reloaded swiftly, and as the slide stripped the top cartridge off the magazine, he triggered the big weapon, killing the man.

Three down, but the doomsday numbers were against the Executioner. Somewhere in the mansion, Richards was on the loose, looking for Cornell. Whether the death dealer could get the assistance of the Rose Initiative recruiter to find the group's deadly secret arsenal or not, it still left a storehouse of Armageddon in untrustworthy hands, and a mass murderer on the loose.

Bolan speared deeper into the mansion's heart, knowing that things were going to get much worse if he didn't act quickly.

MARTIN CORNELL OBSERVED the rampaging battle occurring on his mansion's lawn from his basement control room. Security cameras gave him a godlike view of the conflict going on. He'd come under the focus of two enemy groups, one striking from the front, one from the rear. A sniper armed with a rifle and grenade-launcher combination supported a solitary figure who'd engaged in conflict with a man he recognized as Richards. The two men had broken apart, entering the mansion through separate channels.

The stranger had a window opened up for him by a

grenade launcher. Richards slapped up a low-velocity detonation cord web on another window, which provided a less
spectacular entry hole.

The fighters assembled by his former recruit were
putting up a spectacular assault against the defensive force
provided to him by the Initiative. The invaders were leap-
frogging under cover fire from their partners, using
grenades and their lead van as a tank. Even the Initiative
gunners' M-240 light machine guns weren't able to stop
the armor-plated juggernaut as it finally reached the front
steps, tearing the heavy steel-cored doors off their hinges.
The driver hit Reverse to make room for his allies, and
cleared the doorway just as a defender's AT4 rocket speared
into its side. The tank van was finally stopped cold, split
in two by the armor-piercing, high-explosive warhead.

The damage was already done. The mansion's above-
ground levels were wide open. Cornell sneered.

"They'll be down here soon enough," he said to his
personal protection cadre.

"We'll make it tough for them," an Initiative commando
told him. "Deploy along access Alpha."

Cornell sighed deeply. "It won't stop them."

The cadre commander glared at the old colonel.
"What will?"

"Nerve gas," Cornell stated.

"That will compromise our troops in the upper levels,"
the Initiative man replied.

"For the greater good," Cornell responded. "They're
already finished."

"Bastard," the commander cursed.

"I'm still alive," Cornell told him. He walked toward the
security panel to initiate the gas release when the blast

doors shook violently. Jets of flame penetrated through tiny
tears in the heavy rolled steel barriers.

Cornell snarled. "Atmospheric integrity has been
compromised."

He looked at the commando. "Looks like you get to die
your way anyhow."

The Initiative man grimaced. "Scorched earth, now!"

BOLAN FELT THE FLOOR RUMBLE beneath his feet as an
antitank rocket went off in the basement section. He was
nearing an access door that Spelling had told him would
be Richards's goal. The door was wide open, and an Initiative gunner flopped on the floor. The safety pin of an
antitank rocket was deposited near the man's corpse, con-
firming that Richards had acquired a can opener from the
defensive force.

A team of Richards's gunners opened fire from the
corridor to the living room. Bolan dived behind a large,
heavy antique clock, its bulk blocking the bullets whipping
down the hall toward him. The Executioner saw the
sprawled remains of a trio of Rose Initiative soldiers who'd
tried to stop them, and he knew that he'd join them soon
enough if he didn't make a move. Bolan traded the Desert
Eagle for his M-16/M-203, and thumbed a buckshot shell
into the breech.

The militiamen focused their fire on the clock, their
rounds tearing splinters off the heavy antique as they tried
to get to Bolan. The Executioner poked the cavernous
muzzle of the 40 mm grenade launcher into the hall and
triggered the buckshot shell. The explosive primer charge
took a mass of steel ball bearings and whipped them down
the corridor toward the gunmen at subsonic speeds. The

swarm of pellets separated, spreading into a cone that reached from one wall of the hallway to the other.

The militiamen staked out at the end of the corridor were helpless as the rain of steel tore into their exposed faces and their weapon-filled hands. Corpses were hurled into the living room, flung about like rag dolls. Tattered flesh hung in mangled strips off skulls and forearms, a grisly testament of the effectiveness of the M-203's awesome firepower.

Bolan inserted another buckshot round into his grenade launcher and aimed through the doorway that Richards had taken down to the basement. He pulled the trigger and spit another canister of pelleted death. No one was in the stairwell, but there was a sudden curse from the bottom of the steps. The hard steel balls had ricocheted when they reached the bottom, and some had either struck Richards, or had come close enough to make him sweat.

The Executioner waited for a moment. Richards poked his G-36 up the stairs and cut loose with the assault rifle, suppressed 5.56 mm rounds chewing their way at supersonic speeds to where Bolan would have been if he'd tried to go down the steps too soon. Bolan returned fire with his M-16, but Richards had already ducked behind cover. It was a stalemate, but one that couldn't last forever.

The police had probably received dozens of calls about the war being waged in their midst. With machine guns, grenades and rockets going off, it would only be minutes before the law showed up. Indeed, Bolan expected such a response, but he wanted the enemy taken down before a policeman got caught in the cross fire between Richards's fanatical followers and the Rose Initiative's commando teams.

"Spelling, how are we on wiggle room?" Bolan asked.

"I've got squad cars blocking the access roads," Spelling answered over the radio. "There's about six of them, but they're staying smart and not moving in. Probably waiting for an emergency response team like SWAT."

Bolan thought about it, and knew that undoubtedly Aaron Kurtzman and the Farm team would have been in communication with the authorities. They would have given the cops the warning that they weren't prepared for the kind of hell that was being unleashed at the Cornell estate. Even a SWAT team would be overwhelmed by the kind of reckless firepower being tossed around.

"What about the grounds?" Bolan asked.

"Sporadic movement, and a couple of rounds being fired, but the fight's gone out of both sides," Spelling responded. "I helped with that."

"I'll give you a gold star on your report card," Bolan muttered.

"So he does have a sense of humor." Spelling chuckled.

"Keep both sides contained. I don't want either force trying to make a break and going through some innocent cops," Bolan said, ignoring Spelling's quip. "Are their vehicles out of commission?"

"The vans that didn't get chewed to pieces by the Initiative's machine guns or rockets caught a grenade from me. I've also put an incendiary round into the garage. No one's getting any wheels out of there," Spelling stated. "If they make a break, they're going on foot."

"Good work. Pin down anyone that tries," Bolan said.

"You in the basement?" Spelling asked.

"No. But Richards is caught between me and Cornell's control center," Bolan replied. "Know if there's a back door that he can take?"

"Cornell wouldn't build a safe room without a bolt-hole. But be careful, he'll use nerve gas to make the approach inhospitable," Spelling cautioned.

"Richards popped off an AT4 at the blast doors," Bolan returned. "Now I know why. He broke the seals on Cornell's bunker, making nerve gas a suicide option."

The Executioner heard the rattle of automatic weapons coming from the hallway down below. "He's engaging Cornell's security force. I'm in motion."

Bolan cut communication to Spelling and charged down the steps. He couldn't tell Richards's exact position, but judging from the spray of bullets hammering into the wall at the base of the stairs, he must have been close by.

The Executioner came to a halt at the base of the steps, then glanced around the corner using a pocket mirror.

A small electronic device and an attendant speaker was churning out the noise of an assault rifle firing on full auto, a powerful LED strobe atop the recorder recreating the muzzle-blast. Every thirty rounds, there was the loop of the rifle being reloaded, in sync with the strobe stopping. There was enough swirling smoke in the tunnel, and a propped up corpse sitting behind the device, a rifle jutting from under its armpit, to be a convincing distraction.

The return fire from the control room, however, was letting up. Bolan angled the mirror so that he could see the blast doors, stressed openings allowing him to see into Cornell's command center. There was one gunman still blasting away, his bullets punching into the propped-up corpse, and he screamed, cursing the body that wouldn't fold over and die. Bolan triggered his M-203, its buckshot round sending a concussion wave of rounded steel death through the firing port. He doubted that Richards would be caught in the blast, but he hoped that the last of the Rose Initiative bodyguards would have been taken out by the cone of death.

The rifle went silent, slithering through the opening port as its owner released it, dropping to the floor lifeless.

Bolan transitioned to the Desert Eagle and charged into the corridor. An access panel had been torn off the wall, and the Executioner ditched his M-16 so that he could better slither into the passage. The blast doors were tattered and full of holes, but there was no way a man could slip through the vents in the armor plates, even after the impact of an antitank rocket.

This was Richards's path, and Bolan had to crawl quickly in order to catch up with the renegade death dealer.

If he was lucky, he'd reach the command center in time to put down both men. Unfortunately, luck seemed to be on the death dealer's side.

RICHARDS KICKED OPEN the last grate between himself and Martin Cornell, then pulled back, waiting for the inevitable response from his recruiter.

"Come on in, Cam," Cornell said, his voice weary. "You'll get no fight from me."

Richards checked ahead with a pocket mirror to be sure, then emerged into the command center. Cornell was seated in a chair, a .45 in his lap, his lips drawn tightly in a grim line.

"You know what I'm here for," Richards told him.

Cornell nodded. "Revenge."

"You stole my ideals," Richards stated. "I'm taking them back from the Initiative."

"They took my ideals and dreams too, Cam," Cornell replied. "I left a map on the table for you."

Richards looked to the table, his Beretta leveled at Cornell's heart. "The Arsenal."

"Yes," Cornell said. "They sought out people like us. Just enough idealism to love our country, and just enough hate to make us moldable."

"Hate?" Richards asked.

"You, and Winslow, you were products of economic collapse in the South. You were poor, disenfranchised, rendered worthless by a society who only saw you as bigots. So, in accepting the reality of America's hatred for the Southern man, you became what they wanted you to be," Cornell said.

Richards nodded. "Makes sense."

"Winslow, and your partners, they all were picked up. Just the right mentality. The Rose Initiative gave you scapegoats. They leeched everything from you, so that murdering a cop, or blowing away a kid in your path was perfectly acceptable," Cornell told him.

"And you look down on me for that, even after it was you who drilled that into me?" Richards asked.

"No. I'm the same way. Or was. My father was in the Klan. The FBI took a lot of the power out of them in the sixties, tearing away our roots, and my dad, he died in a shootout with the police. The Initiative picked me up, while I was still seething and in pain. They rubbed salt into my spiritual wounds, making me one of their best operatives."

"Why are you telling me this?" Richards asked.

"Because it's time to cull the herd," Cornell stated. "I want you to have the means to change the world. The Rose Initiative only paid lip service to what we believed. But they have the tools to remake society."

Richards smiled, picking up the map and stuffing it into his pocket. "Bless you, Colonel."

A thunderbolt spit from the vent and Richards dived for cover. Cornell was on the floor, firing his 1911 hard and fast into the opening.

"Go! I'll cover you!" the older man bellowed.

The escape hatch to the command center was wide open. Richards dived in, hearing the firefight between .44 Magnum and .45 ACP handguns going on behind him. The death dealer charged on, leaving the carnage behind him.

He had hope now. He was a puppet freed from his strings, and when he was done, the entirety of corruption would be banished to extinction.

11

Mack Bolan fed the Desert Eagle a fresh magazine, then exited the access tunnel, looking at Colonel Martin Cornell, holding his bloody, torn chest. Gray eyes regarded the Executioner as he rose to his full height.

"Where's Richards?" Bolan asked, knowing he didn't have much time.

"He's got twenty seconds on you, and for him, that's enough, even against you," Cornell answered.

"So where's the Arsenal?"

"You think I'll spill that?" Cornell asked. "You won't torture an unarmed, wounded man." The colonel laughed, blood sputtering from his lips. "My boy's forces are ready to cut loose all across this rotten city. Civilians will die by the busload when Weist and the MTJ open up to provide Cam with his distraction."

Bolan narrowed his eyes.

Cornell spit. "I had this planned. I sent my boy a messenger. I got him off the drugs that were rotting his mind."

"And you end up dying," Bolan said. "Or dying faster."

"Cancer. Exposure to all those chemicals… The doctors said I would live a long time, but my body would be ravaged. I'm too strong and healthy to go out quickly," Cornell replied. "Even with one of your .44s in my gut, I'm still able to hold a conversation."

"And you'll eventually tell me where Richards is going," Bolan said.

"Of course," Cornell whispered. "All part of the plan."

"Because the Initiative and you parted ideological paths. But they don't know. You've been quiet, biding your time," Bolan answered. "You've returned to your initial goal of making the world a better place. Except your idea of better means nihilism."

"There will be a short period of chaos when the governments collapse," Cornell stated. "It won't be true anarchy. But it will come."

Bolan took a deep breath. "It won't happen with the crew that Richards has, though. They'd become tyrants with the power he put in their hands."

"And you are my final tool to eliminate such tyranny. A clean slate. I've set the events in motion. I've loosed my dog of war, and then lured you in to clean it up," Cornell said with a chuckle. "You are the true idealist. You will survive and will purge this world of every ounce of poison. I've given you the tools to create a Utopia."

A small flash drive clattered on the floor at Bolan's feet.

"All the files I gave to Cam," Cornell said with a weak smile. He blinked heavily.

"And what do you get out of this?" Bolan asked.

"A cleansed soul," Cornell responded. "Maybe less time in hell."

Bolan picked up the flash drive, then pulled his Desert Eagle. "You planned the death of a billion people who don't mean anyone harm. The end you seek is not justified by genocide."

"We'll see," Cornell whispered. He lunged at Bolan.

The Desert Eagle thundered, and Cornell went to his

judgment. Bolan turned and left the charnel house. Richards was on his way to loose the forces of extinction, and the Executioner had to take out the death dealer before he completed his mission.

SPELLING WATCHED as the Executioner strode out of Cornell's mansion, walking with a purpose. The defector wondered if the man had taken leave of his senses, when suddenly a fireball issued from his hand, a member of Richards's coalition crumpling over a .44 Magnum slug.

"Get the car ready. There's nothing left here that's a threat," Bolan said, for both Spelling and the Farm to hear. "Send in the cops."

"Gotcha, Striker," Kurtzman's voice growled over the radio link.

Bolan continued toward Spelling's position, and the defector dropped a knotted rope down to the Executioner.

"What's up?" Spelling asked when Bolan reached him.

Bolan looked at the defector for a moment. "Were you in on Cornell's plan?"

"What?" Spelling asked.

The Desert Eagle scythed in an arc, the heavy, blunt barrel clipping Spelling across the chin, dumping him off the top of the wall and into the bushes below. Bolan dropped down, a glare in his cold eyes that burned into Spelling's heart like the coldness of space. Spelling clenched his jaw, realizing that the warrior's fury had bubbled forth again.

"I don't like being played. You and Cornell were pretty clever, using me to clean your house," the Executioner snarled. He leveled the muzzle of the Magnum cannon at Spelling again. "You stepped up the antagonism to keep me from noticing, but things fell into line just too damned neatly."

"How else were we going to get you to do what needed to be done?" Spelling asked.

"A puppet string not acting like you were pulling me along. Finding every hot button I had. That must have taken a lot of research," Bolan said. He holstered the Desert Eagle.

"He had the file on you. Had intel of a John Phoenix doing secret government operations," Spelling explained. "I didn't think you were still alive. Every report has you as dead. Even the CIA kill orders on you were erased. And that takes some work."

"Cornell set it up so that Richards would run into every possible snafu in Los Angeles, to the point of breaking his loyalty to the Initiative," Bolan said. "This was meant to draw me out too."

"We'd been picking up rumors about a super secret government commando solving critical international incidents. You're the only one who could bring Cam down," Spelling said. "It was the perfect ploy. Engineer the end of the corruption of the Initiative, take out the government that turned their back on us, and eliminate the enemies of our nation."

"You couldn't be sure that your preengineered fall would end up with a proper guardian. When you became aware that I was around, though, you knew that you had a chance," Bolan said.

Spelling nodded. "Imagine it. You get to have your perfect world."

"A perfect world?" Bolan repeated. "One where innocents have been slaughtered en masse? How is that perfect?"

"It's a chance to start over again. We're hitting the reset button on history," Spelling told him. "You'll watch the watchmen. When the governments of the world put themselves back together, you'll have to take a more active approach. You'll weed out those among them who are the worst. You'll be able to act with impunity, establishing a rule of law and civilization that today's politicians are too cowardly to enact."

Bolan grabbed Spelling by the wrist and hauled him to his feet. "The reset button doesn't get pushed. There are too many good people out there fighting to make improvements for you to throw it all away in a fit of rage."

"But—"

Bolan shook his head. "Again, you and Cornell thought you knew me. And you're wrong. We're stopping Richards, and the Initiative will go down."

"It would be perfect," Spelling whimpered. "We get rid of the useless—"

Bolan gave Spelling a hard shove toward the car. "The only useless person I see right now is you. Now get behind the wheel."

Spelling staggered along.

THE SUN ROSE OVER WASHINGTON as Cameron Richards stood at the Lincoln Memorial, looking at the tribute to the murdered president. The stone figure was large and impassive, gazing over the city he had watched over as a nation writhed in turmoil, rebelling against itself, turning brother against brother.

Richards felt the sting in his eyes as he realized that his own world had split asunder. Inside him, there was a civil war, between the betrayed young man who had seen his goals crushed underfoot by the machinations of an inhuman juggernaut, and the grown warrior who had been betrayed even by the man who had given him the tools to restore those ideals.

An old man in a uniform saw him. Richards tensed, but the man didn't have a gun on his belt. At the most, he had a flashlight that hung in a ring attached to it. He had his hands tucked into his pockets and he let out a soft sigh.

"You'd be surprised," the man said.

"About what?" Richards asked.

"People who come here. Looking for his guidance."

Richards frowned.

"I never was a churchgoing man, but you get a sense of reverence from this place," the security guard stated. "As if there were a bit of his spirit trapped in the marble."

"Has he ever talked to you?" Richards asked.

The guard looked up into the white marble face of the long lost president. "No. He's never spoken, not out loud. But when I've been looking for an answer, I sometimes stop here, and it comes to me."

Richards nodded. "I wonder what he would have done today. It's as if the country's coming apart at the seams. Every day, I look at the signs, and the people around me are oblivious to it."

The guard took a deep breath. "He went to war to keep the nation from falling apart. To him, there were no acceptable losses. Sure, some folks feel as if it were an illegal attack on a sovereign nation, but it wasn't that simple. People aren't black or white, northern or southern. Those are artificial classifications. He looked at men on both sides and saw Americans."

Richards looked up at the face. "So many died. Cities burned. Families were destroyed."

"It's a hard burden, to do the right thing, no matter the cost," the guard stated. "So many died, but more lived. The country grew and flourished after the war.

Men were on the path to becoming equals, despite rank or skin color."

Richards looked down at his feet. A pang stuck through his gut. He realized that the Rose Initiative had taken his innate bigotry and used it as the leash through which they could pull him through the world. The pang expanded, turning into a rupturing hole in his chest, and he wondered if it weren't the statue at work, the spirit of the great president crushing his soul out of revenge for all the hate inside of him. He took a step back, unsteady.

The guard reached for him, preventing his topple off the steps.

"You've got something on your mind," the guard stated.

"Do you really believe that?" Richards asked.

"Believe what?"

"That the destruction caused by the Civil War…that it led to a better nation," Richards said. "That despite all the loss, the gains made were more important."

The guard looked up at the statue. "Yes. The Union and the Confederacy would have weighed each other down. The hostility needed to break. It was like an infection, a cyst that needed to be lanced and drained."

Richards turned and sat down. He looked at the folded sheaf of papers in his hand.

"What do you have there?" the guard asked.

"A lance," Richards stated. "To drain the infection poisoning the heart of a nation."

The guard nodded. "You're a reporter?"

Richards didn't answer. "If I use this, right here, the country will turn against itself. The whole world will be changed."

"All it takes for evil to flourish is for good men to do

nothing," the guard said. "If you have something that can expose and destroy corruption, then you can't hide it. Not if you love your country."

Richards felt a tear glide down his cheek. "I have to do my duty. Not to do so would mean that the country would lose itself to its own rot."

The guard smiled.

"Thank you."

"Don't thank me," the old man said. "Sometimes people just need a little push in the right direction." He turned and walked away.

Richards took a deep breath, then pulled out his phone.

"Costell? I've got what I need. We're moving on the Arsenal tonight."

"IT'S ENCRYPTED, STRIKER," Kurtzman said as he plugged the thumb drive into his laptop. Sitting in his wheelchair, the computer genius's bushy curls were buffeted by the rotor wash of the helicopter that had landed at the Farm. "Whoever did it is good, because it will take hours to get through it all."

The Executioner's brow was furrowed. Spelling was in manacles, braced by a pair of grim, heavily armed blacksuits "We don't have hours, Bear. Richards has this information in unscrambled format. Tell me that you have a back door."

"Barb, Hunt and Carmen have been poring over potential locations, trying to triangulate increased coded transmissions or altered power usage," Kurtzman replied. He glanced at Spelling, his bushy jaw setting hard. "We're free to discuss this in front of him?"

"He'll be the one to narrow down our choices," Bolan responded. "Pull them up."

"No. Why should I tell you?" Spelling asked.

Kurtzman could see the wave of revulsion rumble through the Executioner. Anyone with less emotional discipline would have been on top of Spelling, beating the information out of him. Bolan's eyes snapped open and he turned, his voice calm, yet cold and hollow.

"I'm done playing games, Spelling. You'll talk."

Winslow Spelling's shoulders jerked in suppressed laughter. "You're not going to torture me, and chemical interrogation would take too long. You're on Cornell's timetable. You'll be just too late to stop the end of life as you—"

Kurtzman flinched as the Executioner's fist crashed up under Spelling's chin. The force of the blow lifted the bound captive from his feet before he toppled into a pile of twisted limbs. The Executioner drew his Desert Eagle and leveled the muzzle at Spelling's head.

"Striker!" Kurtzman shouted.

Bolan pushed Spelling onto his back with the toe of his boot, looking down at the stunned prisoner at his feet. "Give me the list, Bear."

Kurtzman watched as the Executioner touched the muzzle of the massive handgun to Spelling's temple, thumb pushing the pickax-shaped safety lever to the off position.

Bolan knelt next to Spelling, grabbing him by the back of his head, making certain that Spelling felt the four pounds of steel hand cannon grinding against his skull. "We're on a very short timetable here. Your cousin is in position to exterminate a billion people in one quick movement, and plunge the remaining population of this planet into a world war that could claim even more lives. You're one man in comparison to everything I've fought and sacrificed to protect. Do you think that I won't endure a little more regret in order to save them?"

"Bluffing," Spelling replied, blood from the gap in his teeth spraying with each breath. "You're too honorable. Besides, that gun doesn't scare me."

Bolan looked at the Desert Eagle, then clicked on the safety. "You're right. One pull of the trigger, and your brains are all over the ground."

He pushed the handgun back into its holster. He reached into his pocket and pulled out a hook-nosed knife. "This works better."

Spelling saw the fury burning in Bolan's eyes and swallowed. "You're still—"

The point ripped up Spelling's cheek, parting skin and muscle. Spelling's eyes went wide with horror and pain.

"I've seen enough of my friends reduced to armless, legless, faceless lumps of meat, yet still live. I've had to put a bullet in them to end the living hell that they'd been trapped in. Their bodies had been destroyed, stripped of everything that would allow them to interact with the rest of the human race," Bolan told the man. "I know every step that can be taken to make you beg me for death, except that you won't be able to, because I'll remove anything that you could communicate with. No lips. No tongue. No eyes. Not even a flare of the nostrils."

"I…" Spelling began. The hooked point of the blade hovered over his eye, and he could feel the sharp point tug at the lid. "Wait!"

"Show us the list," Bolan said.

Kurtzman showed Spelling the laptop screen.

Spelling spilled his guts, and the choices of where Richards could strike narrowed considerably.

The defector glanced to the grim wraith who folded his knife and stuck it back in his pocket. "You're insane," he said.

Bolan tilted his head. "Insane? No. Insane is murdering half a planet to save one country. What I did was an act of desperation to stop that."

"We gave you that world to rebuild…as a beacon of justice," Spelling sputtered.

Bolan shook his head. "I'm already doing my part to rebuild the world. What you're doing is tearing down what I've worked for."

"So mankind continues to rot. Instead of acting decisively to remove the cancer, you let it fester," Spelling returned.

"One problem with your little delusion," Bolan said. "You forgot about all the people who've helped me and who I've helped. All the millions in the struggle to make things better. You might ignore their contribution, but I don't. No matter what delusional gains you can anticipate after a culling of humanity, they can't compare to the work done by people here and now. And for that kind of ignorance, you're already condemned. You'll never see the good in this world, just its problems. I can't think of a worse punishment than that. Take him away."

"We'll take good care of him," Kurtzman said as the blacksuits hauled Spelling away.

Bolan looked at the list that Spelling had narrowed down. "This, here. On the White House grounds."

"It's an access to a government emergency transport service. There are two entrances, one from within the presidential emergency command center in the lower chambers of the White House, and this access tunnel," Kurtzman said.

Bolan frowned. "Can a helicopter land in that clearing?"

"Not Marine One, but maybe the XH-92. Akira, pop me the specs," Kurtzman said.

"Right there," Tokaido answered on the other end of the

voice link. "Yeah. An XH-92 can drop in and bounce right out. And with fast-ropes, they could rappel an entire platoon into that area."

"Bear, have Hal tell the President to spend the day and night at Camp David. I'll try to contain the Militia of Truth and Justice, but Richards might have other options to divert White House security to get those stealth hawks into the grounds."

"I'll get a squad of blacksuits to bolster Secret Service," Kurtzman stated.

"Extra body armor and a full medic team as well," Bolan suggested. "Weist's people don't believe in small-caliber rifles."

"Meanwhile, you've only got an entire militia to deal with," Kurtzman grumbled.

"Hey, someone's got to do it," the Executioner replied.

Aaron Kurtzman whispered a prayer for the big warrior, knowing he'd need it.

12

Carson Kelly didn't consider himself a fool. He knew that the chances of surviving the full-out assault to start that evening, creating a state of chaos across Washington, D.C., were minimal. However, with such a chance to unleash the assemblage of firepower that Weist had acquired for the Militia of Truth and Justice, and to use it in the destruction of established centers of corruption in an orgy of mass devastation, it was too important. This was exactly the goal he and his men had trained their entire lives for. It was going to be the shot that would be heard across the world, the beginning of a new American revolution when tyranny would collapse in on itself.

He walked alongside the rows of vans, pickup trucks and Jeeps that would carry the Militia of Truth and Justice into the fires of history. He had 138 men still left under his command, after the losses in Idaho and those picked up by the law as they drifted across the nation. Armed with heavy machine guns and rocket launchers, the convoy of American steel would roll through central Washington, spitting fire and flame. Kelly stopped, looking toward the Dragon antitank missile set under a tarp. The mighty warhead had the power to break a tank in two, but its multipurpose warhead could also punch through stone and mortar, crushing an office building. A salvo of these launched to the heart of the Internal Revenue Service or the Bureau of Alcohol, Tobacco, Firearms and Explosives would ensure that both agencies would be thrown into the Stone Age due to the loss of their staff and their computerized records. Of course, the real targets were the Rose Initiative, but Richards and Weist would be taking the fight to them in the high-tech XH-92 helicopters. The stealth birds would drop them in the heart of the enemy to begin the culling of the madmen in charge of running the world's greatest nation into the dirt.

Kelly wished that he had been selected for that part of the mission, but putting the jackbooted thugs of the ATF and the IRS on the defensive was an equally vital goal for the plan.

If he had to die, he'd be making his imprint on history using the blood of hundreds of oppressors. Surely, the military and the police would send out entire divisions to contain the mayhem that his valiant, highly trained warriors would release.

A hushed wind transformed into the thunder of a rotor, and Kelly whirled. A powerful-looking, sharklike helicopter hovered over the staging area for the MTJ. Kelly jolted in shock at the sight of the bristling gunship, hanging over the bastion of his army, and rushed toward a pickup truck to grab a Stinger missile.

"So, you figured out where we were!" Kelly shouted. "And you called in an air strike on us?"

He hauled the Stinger missile to his shoulder. Dozens of his men surged toward the parked convoy, hoping to grab heavy weapons to blow the enemy craft out of the sky, but *Dragonslayer* sliced into the air, rising into the sky until it was a mere dot.

Kelly tried to track the battle copter, but even the target screen couldn't get a good lock on it.

"What…" one of his men grumbled, confused. "What's going on?"

"Only one helicopter?" Kelly murmured. "And it ran off. Where the hell is the army? Or the Air Force?"

A hollow thump sounded in the distance, and the assembled militiamen whirled. They saw a man disappear behind cover, but they didn't realize that their fully fueled, fully armed convoy was a big, explosive target to a determined soldier with a grenade launcher.

The M-203 High Explosive Dual-Purpose grenade dropped out of the sky and landed in one of the MTJ's borrowed vans, and Kelly, seeing the slow-moving blooper round in flight, realized that the target was packed with portable light rocket launchers. The disposable warheads, and the gasoline in the van were sparked off by several ounces of C-4.

Kelly felt the concussion wave strike him, and he was lifted off his feet by the torrential wind. His Stinger missile toppled off his shoulder and clattered in the dirt, as fingers of flame, tipped with talons of shredded metal, sliced through the air over his head. As he fell under the force of the explosion, he saw one of those flaming streaks of metal strike a fellow militiaman in the center of his face.

Around him, other men screamed as their flaming doom rained on them with lethal results. Kelly howled in shock and crawled through the dirt. His hand fell to the .45 automatic pistol on his hip, his only weapon since he'd traded his rifle for the Stinger missile. A handgun was nothing in comparison to the one-man artillery barrage provided by the grenade launcher. Kelly rolled onto his back and trig-

gered the .45 anyway, screaming in defiance of the
incoming hail of death pouring down onto his men.

THE EXECUTIONER KNEW that things would go easier if he
had Grimaldi simply lay down a full storm of machine-gun
and rocket fire against the Militia of Truth and Justice, but
Dragonslayer might eventually be needed elsewhere. He
couldn't risk a lucky shot from an antimatériel rifle or a
rocket launcher damaging the sleek combat aircraft when
all of its sensors and combat abilities might be called upon
to deal with whatever other threats Cameron Richards
sought to unleash upon the unsuspecting capital.

Besides, given how the enemy had concealed its
vehicles under camouflage netting, bunched closely
together and outfitted with all manner of high explosives,
the motor yard was a sweet, fat target. Dozens of men had
raced toward the vehicles when Grimaldi let them hear the
floating war shark's engines for a brief second after Bolan
had rappelled into position. Some of them were down, but
most of them had seen, or had been informed, of the Executioner's presence by their allies. Rifle and handgun fire
cracked into the hillside around Bolan as he triggered a
second 40 mm shell into a pickup truck. The vehicle split
in two, its eruption flipping over two Jeeps, depositing
their bulk onto the militia gunmen using them for cover.

With practiced skill, Bolan reloaded the M-203, snapped
it shut and fired again. A militiaman had crawled into the
back of a Jeep and was trying to fumble a belt into the feed
of a machine gun. He looked up in horror as the 40 mm
shell struck his mounted weapon. The tripod bent wildly,
and the frame of the heavy machine gun vaulted violently
through the gunner's chest, killing him.

The blast wave from the HEDP round broke apart the linked .50-caliber ammunition belt, spraying its cartridges around at about one third of their usual velocity. Considering that at full power, a .50 BMG bullet could tear through a pickup truck as if it were made of paper, the full-sized cartridges at reduced velocity tore through man and machine with shredding effect.

Bolan had another 40 mm shell in the breech as he spotted a line of gunmen scrambling out of their temporary barracks to rush his position. The Executioner aimed at the leader of the throng and fired. When the HEDP round smashed into his rib cage, its detonator was activated.

Bolan brought his hand back to the trigger of the M-16 and followed up the initial cone of devastation wrought by his grenade launcher with a rapid-fire burst of 5.56 mm bullets that broke the charge against his position. With half a dozen bodies strewed at the base of the hill he was on, the remainder of the strike force limped back toward their cover.

Bolan slammed a buckshot round into place and fired. The sheet of ball bearings that erupted from the muzzle of the grenade launcher hammered onto one of the flanks of homegrown terrorists, shredding bodies. More autofire anchored those who had avoided the initial swathe of destruction as the suddenly disorganized militia resistance fired wildly to cover their own retreat.

Burning fuel cooked off the tanks of neighboring vehicles in the convoy's lot. The wheeled armada fell victim to its own light weight and oversupplied nature. They hadn't been expecting an artillery barrage to hammer them, especially when the vehicles were huddled together. Bolan spared another HEDP round to lance into the heart of another knot of pickups and Jeeps, exploding ammunition and rockets and blazing gasoline spreading. The camouflage netting over the top of the secreted motor pool had caught fire in several places, and the flames were racing through the netting itself, dropping hot, melted nylon clumps onto screaming men who had neglected to get fully dressed as they rushed to their vehicles. Other hot polymer embers started fires in the Jeeps and the beds of the pickups, tarps catching flame to the point where the rocket launchers they concealed detonated under the heat. Secondary explosions rocked the armada of vehicles and the militiamen who had rushed into their midst to try to fight the fires, recover their arsenal of heavy weaponry, or to even drive the vans and pickups out of harm's way before the flames caught hold of them. The smell of roasting flesh wafted on the wind toward the Executioner, telling him that the forces he was battling against were suffering heavy casualties that weren't directly attributable to him.

Bolan fired an HEDP into the heart of one of the barracks buildings, an old cabin. The log construction of the structure detonated, jagged splinters and chunks of bark flying. The powerful concussion turned the cabin into a kill zone, and none of the militia gunners who'd taken up positions at the windows survived. It was ruthless combat, but the Executioner knew that each of the men he was pitted against had no compunctions about opening fire on a building full of noncombatants.

Bolan knew that if he was to have a chance of sparing the lives of the citizens of Washington, D.C., then he was going to have to put out every ounce of firepower he carried. His load-bearing vest was festooned with various shells for the 40 mm grenade launcher, spare magazines clipped to a thigh pouch. He loaded up another buckshot round and triggered it at another cabin. The steel pellets blew through the windows that a squad of militia riflemen had taken up a position in, chopping through heads, weapons and hands in a blistering wave of flesh-rending death. Pellets bounced off the log front of the cabin and peppered gunmen who were crossing by the cabin under the cover fire of their compatriots. The inelasticity of the steel bearings kept them from losing any momentum as they rebounded, clawing MTJ gunmen and leaving them bloody, ravaged forms. The few survivors gave out feeble cries for medical attention, but none would be coming.

The Executioner plunked a fragmentation shell into the midst of the wounded survivors, the detonation removing the militiamen's pain with a single burst of explosive force.

He then stuffed another HEDP round into the M-203 and snapped off the round toward a burning van, making it disappear in an orange blossom of flame. High-explosive ordnance stored in its back magnified the detonation. Pickup trucks pinwheeled, one unlucky rifleman smashed into bloody paste as a tumbling vehicle rocketed over him.

The concentrated hail of autofire from the militia, a torrential rain of burning lead that made the hillside around Bolan's cover a devastating kill zone, had diminished. Gunmen were on the run, terrified of the lone warrior who'd visited hell upon them. Others were dead or wounded, while those who had taken up positions of cover that weren't blown to pieces, held their fire, fearful of drawing the wrath of the Executioner. Bullets sang across the space between the campground cabins and the blazing motor pool and Bolan's sniper roost, but no longer with the intensity of more than a hundred men fighting for their cause.

Like many fanatics, first contact with real opposition

had shattered their spirit. The lethal rain of explosive doom and trained marksmanship that cleaned up the battlefield had taken the fight out of a group of terrorists, revealing them for the opportunistic cowards that they truly were.

Striding into the open, Bolan fired precision bursts at positions that reacted to his appearance. His 72-grain match hollowpoint rounds homed in on muzzle-flashes, finding unprotected faces and foreheads. Using lateral movement, his senses sharp and unhampered by the rollicking explosions that had rolled across the battleground, Bolan had the advantage over his foes, choked and blinded by smoke, and deafened by being too close to grenade detonations. Targeting the enemy by muzzle-flashes, taking range and bullet drop into account, the experienced sniper met panic fire with marksmanship. Those who gave away their positions gave their lives away, Bolan targeting them with a short burst of autofire.

Even when a half-blind, shell-shocked rifleman tried to adjust for the Executioner's old position, the warrior wound down the hillside in a serpentine pattern, taking advantage of every piece of cover he could slip behind. Following Bolan was difficult, and when they did get a free shot at him, the militamen's bullets were stopped cold by a tree trunk.

Upon meeting with a real soldier, the terrorists had been slapped in the face with a cold and deadly reality. The Militia had found Justice, and in so doing, had learned that the Truth of their ideals was actually a hollow, empty lie.

CARSON KELLY LIMPED, dragging his broken leg as he struggled to get away from the Executioner's handiwork. He was choking on smoke and more than a few of his own

tears. He'd passed by wrecked, savaged bodies that had
been split open by shearing metal, or crisped, charred
skeletons, human beings reduced to carbonized ash as
flaming gasoline had immolated them completely. His
hearing was half gone, blood pouring from a ruptured
eardrum. He used a jammed rifle as a crutch to help him
limp along, his shattered leg dangling useless behind him.

Kelly stumbled and fell. The agony that jarred his
broken leg filled his throat with bile, and he gagged,
heaving in order to keep from choking to death.

"We had all the guns. We had the missiles. We had the
plan. We had God on our side," he whimpered.

"No, you didn't" a voice cut through the crackle of
flames behind him. Kelly glanced over his shoulder, and
stared wide-eyed at the man, looming over him. His load-
bearing vest had several deflated pockets on it. In his hands
was a rifle and grenade launcher combination, but it wasn't
aimed at him.

Cold, deadly eyes pinned him in place even more effec-
tively than if the man had a boot pressed against his
snapped thigh. Kelly swallowed hard.

"This was supposed to be our greatest battle," Kelly
whimpered.

"It wasn't," Bolan said.

Kelly pressed his forehead into the dirt. "We were
supposed to go down, fighting the Army, fighting the cops.
We were supposed to end the age of oppression in a hail
of bullets. It would have been glorious."

"All it took was one man to take out the trash," Bolan
replied.

"One man," Kelly gasped.

"Can't say I'm sorry I stripped you of your dream,"

Bolan told him. "But then, no sane man would have had such a dream."

Kelly's tears soaked the dirt beneath him. His fingers clawed up clumps, and he could feel his nails breaking, pulling out at their roots. The pain in his leg was horrendous.

"Are there any more groups working with Richards?" Bolan asked. "Like the Appalachian White Coalition?"

Kelly shook his head. "They only sent a few men. He only used them to get into Cornell's mansion."

"He wouldn't have told you where the helicopters were, would he?" Bolan asked.

"No," Kelly muttered. "You're not going to shoot me, are you?"

"You're not armed. You're hurt. You're no threat, just a pathetic, broken piece of wreckage. And you're lucky. The racket we raised, there'll be a hundred cops and ambulances to gather up your little toy soldiers and put them back together again. You'll all meet up in a jail cell."

Kelly looked up, pleading. "I want some dignity…"

Bolan stared at him for a long moment, then pulled the Beretta from his shoulder holster, tossing it to Kelly. He slung the M-16 over his shoulder. "Fill your hand."

Kelly smirked and lunged for the Beretta, looking at the Executioner's hand as it blazed swiftly down to the massive handgun strapped to his thigh.

The roar of Bolan's Desert Eagle was the last sound he ever heard.

THE EXECUTIONER STOOPED and picked up his Beretta, wiping it off and putting it back in its holster. He put the Desert Eagle away as well. No one had gathered up the courage to fire a shot at him in over a minute. He keyed his communicator, contacting the Farm.

"What's the damages?" Bolan asked.

"We've got thirty bodies racing through the woods, and another fifteen curled up in holes around the campgrounds," Kurtzman replied. "Satellite and infrared imaging confirms that the survivors have dumped their weapons. When the cops come in, they'll have an easy time picking up the pieces. "

"ETA?" Bolan inquired.

"You've got five minutes," Kurtzman answered.

"Jack?" Bolan called.

"Coming in for pickup," Grimaldi said.

"Good. Because this isn't finished by half." Bolan sighed.

Dragonslayer swung over the bloody campground, dropping a winch line to pick up the Executioner.

13

Costell looked from the police scanner to Cameron Richards, concern darkening his face. "No more Militia of Truth and Justice," he announced grimly.

"They were the icing on the cake. They won't expect us to make our move now," Richards stated.

"The Initiative isn't going to be fooled," Costell responded. "Our only advantage is the fact that the man pursuing you doesn't know where we'll be accessing the Arsenal, or even where its exact location is."

"Maybe," Richards said.

Costell tilted his head.

"He got into Cornell's mansion. He might have gotten the information out of the old man," Richards replied. "We're operating on borrowed time."

The cell phone burbled. Richards picked it up and opened the screen. It was a text message from one of Weist's scouts: Marine One leaving.

Richards's eyes clenched shut and he showed the message to Costell. The man was his pilot, lifelong friend and closest confidant. Together, they had braved countless forays into the darkness of the world, engaging in battle with the worst that humankind had to offer. Richards didn't have to break it down for Costell to understand. The experienced fighter nodded grimly.

"The White House will be empty tonight," Costell said.

"It doesn't mean that the security forces on hand won't be ready to greet us with a wall of bullets," Richards murmured. "Without the distractions provided by the MTJ, we're stuck with our own devices."

"That's why we kept them so far away from our true strike force," Costell admitted. "A half-dozen car and truck bombs, across the city, ready to go on a simple cell-phone signal."

Richards nodded. Cobbling together high-powered explosives, leftover munitions from artillery units, each car and truck bomb was assembled from six 155 mm Howitzer shells bundled together. The combined explosive power of the shells, wrapped in the relatively fragile outer shell of a sedan or tractor trailer, would create blast craters twenty feet deep and hundreds of feet around. The two tractor trailers had double-packs of Howitzer shells, and had chunks of scrap iron piled up all around the shells. The scrap iron would be launched from the trailers at lethal velocities, spreading death and destruction even farther around the improvised doomsday devices.

The city would be shaken like it hadn't been since the Civil War. The bombs were strategically placed in order to make the most of civilian losses. They wanted ambulances and squad cars clogging the streets, and emergency rooms filled to the bursting point. Emergency services had to be dealing with thousands of casualties, fires and other mayhem. That would make the two stealth helicopters harder to track, thanks to news helicopters and police and fire department aircraft in the air.

Dropping in on the White House grounds would be made easy by the high-tech transport ships. Between their distraction tactics and the electronic measures to muffle audio, radar and infrared signatures, the XH-92s would be as hard to track as ghosts. With each bird stuffed with a dozen trained commandos, each handpicked by Colonel Jacob Weist, Richards would have the manpower on hand to deal with whatever the Rose Initiative had waiting for him at the Arsenal.

"Once you drop us off, get the hell out," Richards said. "Find a spot to hide out. Mexico. Someplace. I'll track you down if I make it."

"If you make it?" Costell asked. "This isn't a suicide mission."

"With the White House having the heads-up about our coming there, we're looking at some bad odds," Richards said.

Costell shook his head.

"Suit up. We're doing this in broad daylight," Richards told him. "They won't be expecting us to push the time-table up, especially if they've broken any of the MTJ."

Costell nodded. "We can pull this off."

Richards smiled as his partner left the room.

COLONEL NELSON STORM looked like hell as his face appeared on the monitor in the Stony Man War Room. Still recovering from injuries, he wasn't in any condition to travel, but appearing on web cam enabled him to be part of the solution. Emily Walters sat next to Storm, looking a little healthier than the last time Bolan had met with her.

"Sorry to cut into your recuperation, sir," Bolan apologized. "But we need everything we can to get an advantage over the XH-92 thieves."

"What kind of terrain will they be flying over?" Storm asked.

"Urban environment," Bolan replied.

"How urban?" Storm asked. "Amid tall buildings, you're in for a nightmare. The XH-92 was designed for city fighting. With an eight-bladed rotor for extra lift surface, the diameter it requires to fly safely is dramatically reduced. It can go where other helicopters can't for fear of hard contact with buildings."

"A low-lying city setup. Washington, D.C.," Bolan told him.

"Even there, we've taken into account layouts such as Baghdad. It can operate at full speed, hovering only ten feet off the pavement, and take advantage of low-lying buildings for cover," Storm answered. "The thing has nap of the Earth avoidance systems that allow it to cut down a freeway at 180 miles an hour, in full traffic, and still avoid crashing into trailer trucks."

"Are there any built-in systems that would allow for tracking?" Bolan asked. "Something we can hack into?"

Storm glanced to Walters. She nodded.

"Dr. Reader had concerns about the potential of the XH-92 falling into the wrong hands. He had a passive sensor built into one of the interior panels. It can be activated with a certain code. It has to be activated by a transmission over emergency frequency, and only using the code. Otherwise, the XH-92 would be visible, which defeats the purpose of the stealth craft," Storm stated. "Unfortunately, up until recently, I was too out of it to even remember the code."

"You've been through a lot," Bolan said. "Painkillers for your injuries…"

Storm winced. "Thanks for the sympathy, soldier, but you need the code."

He gave it.

Hunt Wethers broadcast the code across the emergency frequencies.

Bolan's eyes turned toward the map of the Washington, D.C., metropolitan area. Two blips raced across the map, spearing directly toward the White House.

"Bear! Put an electronic damper over the city now!" the Executioner bellowed. "Jack! Fire up *Dragonslayer!*"

Bolan raced into the hallway. He had his radio hooked up, and spoke through the hands-free microphone. "They'll try to distract emergency services from their true goal. Are the blacksuits in place?"

"Yes, Striker," Kurtzman answered. "We have reports of a single car bomb detonating a moment before we sent out the jamming signal. There haven't been any other detonations."

"Sequential firing, to maximize the damage," Bolan said as he charged up the stairs. He burst out of the main farmhouse, where Jack Grimaldi idled with *Dragonslayer,* its rotors whirling, engines at full power. "Reports?"

"Twenty fatalities as of the first estimate," Kurtzman answered grimly.

Bolan hauled himself into the shotgun seat of the helicopter, and Grimaldi pulled up on the stick, lancing the sleek battle copter into the midafternoon sky. Kicking in the full throttle, Grimaldi pushed the lady to her full 200 mph. Kurtzman keyed in the telemetry from the Farm's satellite view to a readout panel on *Dragonslayer.*

"They'll know that we've got eyes on them," Grimaldi noted. "Once those transmitters go live, their electronic countermeasures will pick up the signal."

"I figure a minute until they're at the White House. And

we've got four minutes until we get there," Bolan stated, looking at the monitor.

"Three minutes," Grimaldi said. "That's a long time for the Secret Service and the blacksuits to deal with any problems."

"Striker!" Kurtzman announced. "We've got aerial contacts. Missile launches over the city!"

"Antiaircraft missiles." Bolan's face tightened in concern. "A missile hits one of those birds over a populated area, and we've got all kinds of civilian casualties."

"And if the missile doesn't hit, our buddies at the White House end up facing two stealth helicopters at once," Grimaldi grumbled.

Bolan watched the screens as Richards's helicopters swerved, going into evasive maneuvers to avoid the lethal antiaircraft missiles. For the sake of the unsuspecting citizens beneath the deadly dance of missile and helicopter, Bolan prayed that the enemy pilots were good enough to minimize the damage.

HENRY COSTELL CRANKED the stick as the first of the SAM missiles rocketed toward the XH-92 stealth helicopter. The smoke contrail billowed up to engulf the windshield, but Costell's lightning reflexes had given him just enough of an edge to keep the murderous warhead inches from contacting the aircraft. The hull of the bird was radar absorbent enough to make the proximity detonator mounted in the nose of the spearing SAM useless. It zipped past the XH-92 and struggled to make a hairpin turn, homing in on the small radio transmitter that had betrayed the craft's presence to the Rose Initiative. The SAM struggled, its engine flaring out as its ailerons tried to make the about-face.

The missile was designed to chase high-speed aircraft

like jets, which required long distances to make turns. The helicopter did a fast drop in altitude, and the SAM, in its struggle to keep up, didn't pick up the presence of a billboard between it and its target. The impact fuse crumpled, detonating its warhead, spraying the street below with debris. Only the rooftop the billboard was mounted upon protected the citizens on the sidewalk from a rain of shrapnel that would have slain them.

Weist's pilot, Jeff O'Neil, pulled similar evasive maneuvers, doing everything to put structures between his bird and the white, rocket-motored arrow that sought to take it down. More missiles rose in the distance, from secreted launchers around the Washington, D.C., area, the white plumes of their engine contrails arcing.

"I'm counting a half-dozen missiles this time," Costell said. "Like it or not, Thorn knows we're coming."

"Electronic countermeasures activated," Richards replied, focusing on his mission. Costell's drastic course corrections to avoid the SAMs had knocked them off schedule. They should have been at the White House grounds half a minute ago, but the aerial duel had eaten up time. "I'm jamming everything in the area."

Costell gave the console a punch. "Looks like you got rid of that transmission signal."

"Too late now," Richards stated. "We've got the enemy's attention."

"Rebel One," O'Neil announced. "I've got a visual on a fast-moving helicopter coming in."

"Estimated time of arrival?" Costell asked.

"It's coming in at over two hundred miles per hour," O'Neil said. "Looks like we've got even more of a reprieve than we thought."

Richards pointed out the windshield. The SAMs had picked up a new target, having been blinded to the presence of the darting stealth birds. They swung around toward the fast-moving enemy helicopter that had popped up on their tail.

"This is almost too easy," Richards said. "Get to the access now!"

Costell throttled up his bird, popping it over the low rooftops, aiming the XH-92 toward the White House.

"WELL, LOOKS LIKE WE don't have to worry about an XH-92 going down in flames," Grimaldi said.

"Taking control of the GECAL," Bolan replied.

Grimaldi knew that it was the only option. The SAMs were speeding too close to civilian air traffic. The mighty .50-caliber multibarreled machine gun was the only thing that could take out the enemy SAMs, and even then, it would take all of the Executioner's skill and accuracy to take them down.

Bolan put the crosshairs on the closest of the SAM rockets as it streaked across the sky, its white-dart core surrounded by a halo of flame and trailing smoke as its solid fuel engine propelled it to near supersonic speeds. Bolan caressed the trigger, sending out a churning storm of heavyweight rounds. Since the missile was several hundred feet over the city, its explosion wouldn't cause much damage. The powerful 700-grain rounds chewed into the antiaircraft missile, splitting it asunder. One round struck through the heart of the warhead, detonating it, but the .50-caliber bullet had already shattered the shrapnel casing around the explosives. Instead of creating a ten-meter-across globe of plane-rending death, the pressure of the detonation simply popped the casing apart like a clamshell.

The rocket motor erupted, its pieces disintegrating under the heat of its own fuel cooking off.

One missile down, five to go. Bolan swiveled the GECAL's barrels toward a second SAM, unleashing a 25-round burst that ground it into a fast-moving cloud of confetti as it broke apart under the assault. Another SAM had gotten much closer, and Grimaldi jerked *Dragonslayer* out of the way of the helicopter-killing rocket. The SAM split the air, roaring past like a freight train. Bolan swung the GECAL around, trying to catch the retreating antiaircraft missile before it went too far away from *Dragonslayer* and picked up a civilian aircraft. He churned out another burst, raking the tail of the missile. Its rocket motor disappeared, vaporizing under the assault. The warhead spun out of the air, tumbling to the ground out of control. The last that Bolan and Grimaldi saw of it was when it detonated in a back alley, a plume of smoke vomiting into the sky from the crash site.

The other three SAMs were closing in, flying in formation. Bolan might have been able to take two out before they hit *Dragonslayer,* but all three were too much for even his marksmanship skills.

Suddenly the SAMs swerved, swinging out toward the coast.

"Striker, sorry about that. It took a few moments to find the override for the SAMs. Are you guys okay?" Kurtzman called over the radio.

"Yeah," Bolan responded. "Just send in some Emergency Response to where that one warhead landed. Chances are that there weren't any people in the alley, but—"

"They're responding," Kurtzman said. "We've got activity at the White House. Security teams on the rooftop are opening fire, but the XH-92s have dropped smoke and tear gas to hinder our boys."

"Hinder?" Bolan asked.

"They came up on a blind side, out of effective range of Secret Service and blacksuit snipers. They seem to be avoiding contact," Kurtzman explained.

"It figures. They're going in low profile to minimize casualties before they get to the Arsenal," Bolan said. "We're a minute out—"

"One of the helicopters has broken ranks. It's heading straight for us," Grimaldi spoke up. The console lit up, a sound that Bolan recognized all too readily. "We've got a radar lock."

"We can't get into a dogfight, Jack," Bolan said. "The weapons on this bird could destroy a building if we miss."

"I know," Grimaldi stated. "Countermeasures kicking in. I'm going to go for the rush. Crawl in back and get ready to rappel out."

Bolan knew that Grimaldi could work all of *Dragon-slayer*'s weaponry on his own. The helicopter was specifically designed to make Grimaldi a one-man air force, capable of dealing with multiple threats the same way Bolan could handle superior numbers of ground troops. He slithered out of his seat and got to the back. Knowing that he was going to have to go into close quarters in the underground tunnel complex, he scooped up his Olympic Arms OA-93 machine pistol, the smallest version of the M-16 ever produced. Capable of firing the full-power 5.56 mm round out of its stubby six-inch barrel, it had enough penetration to shred all but the heaviest body armor. The 40-round magazines and the Aimpoint low-power red-dot scope on top made it an ideal close-quarters weapon. A folding-style shoulder stock, independent of the gas tube poking out of the back of the compact machine pistol, coupled with a vertical pistol grip attached to the barrel sleeve made the weapon easy to control and handle. A blunt, fat suppressor added another few inches to the stubby full-auto chain saw, but Bolan knew he needed it to minimize the blistering muzzle-flash, and to protect his hearing in close quarters. Spare magazines were tucked into pouches on his load-bearing vest.

Bolan hooked the carabiner clip to his belt with one hand as the other clenched a support rung built into the ceiling of *Dragonslayer*. The XH-92 had caught up with the Stony Man war bird, but Jack Grimaldi's flying skills made target acquisition difficult for the enemy pilot. Bolan heard the rattle of a light machine gun, but *Dragonslayer's* armor was too thick for the 7.62 mm rounds from the stealth helicopters. The sneaky birds were meant for minimal contact, and a single M-240 door gun was available on each of them. The machine gun was meant to give support to insertion teams for extraction under fire, the main punch meant to be provided by escort gunships, of the nature of *Dragonslayer* and her GECAL .50 and missile pods.

The Executioner felt the gunship shake, the GECAL hammering out its .50-caliber thunderstorm toward one of the XH-92 helicopters. The use of the craft's rocket launchers would have been problematic, but the .50 was a precision weapon. It could conceivably damage the XH-92, but without shattering it into a dozen flaming pieces capable of taking out a citizen on the street. Bolan trusted Grimaldi's instincts, regardless. Chances were that the streets were being evacuated. In the meantime, the Executioner held on with all of his strength, the muscles in his forearms protesting as g-forces slammed into him. Grimaldi swung the helicopter about in order to keep from firing the GECAL in the direction of bystanders.

Bolan glanced out the window and saw an XH-92 zip past. A greasy smear of dark smoke was dragged across the noonday sky after it, informing him that Grimaldi had scored a hit. It wasn't fatal damage to the stealth helicopter, but the smoldering fuselage was indicative of eventually crippling damage. The second helicopter screamed past *Dragonslayer,* a door gunner hanging on to his machine gun, hammering out long, searing streams of autofire. Grimaldi twisted *Dragonslayer*'s path as the XH-92 got close, avoiding a collision where the nose of the enemy ship would have clipped the rotors of the Stony Man gunship. The GECAL shook the helicopter again, and Bolan knew that it wasn't to tag the craft that had lanced into the sky, climbing into the sun.

He whipped around and saw that Grimaldi was hot on the tail rotors of the other stealth craft, GECAL churning out its brutal war song. Sparks flared on the side of the craft, and it lurched violently, losing power as one engine vomited out an orange smear of flame that darkened into a roiling black cloud. Bolan held tight as Grimaldi accelerated past the hit aircraft, throwing the bulk of *Dragonslayer* into the path of the enemy ship. The pilot pulled up hard on the stick, robbing himself of whatever momentum he had left, and the rotors slowed, dragging the ship to the ground.

"The other one is running like hell," Grimaldi stated.

"Drop me off and then bring him down," Bolan said.

"You know it," Grimaldi answered. He swung the sleek war bird over the White House grounds. A section of lawn

had been torn up by a breaching charge, revealing the shattered hinges of a trapdoor. Bolan scanned out the window,
looking at the White House. While enveloped with various
colors of chemical smoke and tear gas, the great building
was unharmed.

No, Bolan thought. The real goal of Richards wasn't the
President or his command center, but the access tunnel
that would bring him to the doorstep of the Rose Initiative's
arsenal. He launched out the side of *Dragonslayer,* the
rope hooked to his belt slowing his descent enough so that
when he hit the grass, it was a minor jolt, rather than a
bone-breaking impact. With a deft movement, he unhooked
from the fast-rope. Grimaldi swung his chopper into the
sky, charging off in the direction of the other XH-92 stealth
helicopter.

From there on out, the Executioner fought alone.

14

The steps down into the tunnel were covered in broken sod and the twisted remnants of the armored doors that had concealed the secret entrance. Bolan unslung his OA-93 and moved down into the darkness, gripping the stubby assault weapon tightly to his shoulder. He had a solid cheek weld on the folding stock, and the Aimpoint, with its tritium illumination enhancements, made the dim tunnel a readily visible fighting zone. It seemed no booby traps had been left behind to hinder the Executioner's pursuit of the Rose Initiative's renegade death dealer, but Bolan wasn't going to take that at face value. He moved at a quick, but careful pace, fast enough to eat up ground, but not so quick that he wouldn't notice the caress of a nylon trip wire attached to a grenade.

There wasn't any rear security left behind, but given Richards and Weist's need to penetrate into the Arsenal with minimum fuss, as well as their arranged distractions, Bolan guessed that they couldn't afford the manpower. Knowing the capacity of the XH-92 helicopter stealth transports, he was filled with a moment of concern. Twenty-four armed commandos was a large force to take into a facility, which meant that Richards expected to encounter at least fifty Rose Initiative defenders, and perhaps high powered defensive systems as well.

The Executioner was going to be seriously outnumbered.

He knew it wasn't like the assault on the Militia of Truth and Justice. These were trained commandos, both on offense and defense, all well-equipped, and coordinated in their tactics. But, the Executioner knew what to expect from professional fighting men, and he could anticipate their responses to his moves. That had given Bolan the advantage in countless clashes with skilled foes across the globe.

Sweeping the tunnel ahead of him, he saw no opportunity for sabotage. He picked up his pace, running down the long, empty corridor. The fluorescent lights glowed and flickered as he sped past them. There were no doors or pipes, just smooth concrete and cinder-block walls.

As Bolan poured on the speed, he spotted a pair of double doors in the distance. Gunfire rattled, a pair of rifles chattering in response to his footsteps. Bolan threw himself into a face-first slide along the floor. He framed one of the distant gunmen in the optics of the scope and pulled the trigger. The fat suppressor on the stubby machine pistol sputtered as 72-grain match hollowpoint rounds rocketed at high velocity down the tunnel. Bolan had aimed high, anticipating the reduced barrel length limiting the range of the OA-93. In the distance, Bolan's trio of 5.56 mm rounds snapped into the enemy gunner's chest, body armor shredding under the onslaught of the extra-heavy rounds. Unfortunately for Bolan, the rounds didn't have much killing power at seventy-five yards after coming into contact with Kevlar.

Bolan changed tactics. He focused on the legs of two men, sweeping them with a magazine-draining burst. The commandos tried to tag him, but with Bolan prone on the floor, their lowered aim was off. Bullets hammered into the concrete ahead of him, ricocheting over his head and shoulders. He fired straight ahead, and the 40-round magazine's remaining payload emptied, tearing through knees, shins and thighs. The knee guards and boots of the two commandos provided some protection, but the muscles and bones of his enemies' legs were all too vulnerable. The pair collapsed in agony. Bolan pushed himself to his feet and raced to the end of the corridor, his weapon trained on the pair in case they recovered from their shock and injuries to continue the fight.

One man was pale, his limp form lying in a lake of his lifeblood. A round from Bolan's OA-93 machine pistol had severed the femoral artery in his left leg, and he had bled to death within a few moments. The other gunman was curled up in agony, his legs bloody masses of twisted bone and muscle. The man was scrambling to reach his fallen rifle. Bolan drew his Desert Eagle and fired a single shot into the base of the fatally wounded commando's neck. The .44 Magnum round shattered his spine and ripped out the lower part of his brain, bringing his suffering to a swift end.

With that bit of butcher's work complete, Bolan stepped carefully through the gateway the men had guarded. Two pairs of train tracks stretched off into the distance.

A train car sat on one of the tracks. There was room for another one, but it had to have disappeared into the distance. The Executioner plucked a pair of binoculars from his battle vest and saw that the tunnel extended for several miles.

Bolan climbed into the train car, but his worst fears were confirmed. The controls to the train had been wrecked by a blast of gunfire. He got out of the car and saw that the tracks ahead of the car had been blown into twisted fragments by a grenade. Richards had made certain that no one was going to easily pursue him.

"I'm not finished yet," Bolan said as he scanned the tunnel. He spotted a boarded-up area and used his combat knife to pry an opening. His flashlight swept the darkness, and he saw an old pickup truck, its wheels adapted for riding along train tracks. He entered the maintenance bay, looking for some gasoline, hoping that the battery would still work on the old truck.

RICHARDS SLOWED THE TRAIN CAR as it neared the end of its trek, five miles under the streets of Washington, D.C. He turned to Weist, and the commando and his forces moved to the doors, pushing them open. One jammed a pry bar into the mechanism, locking it open, and the fighting men disgorged from the train car.

"You sure?" Weist asked.

"My mission, my risk," Richards responded "Go. I need to soften up the enemy."

Weist nodded and leaped out the held-open doors.

Richards slammed the throttle to full speed, then jammed a screwdriver into the control, keeping the dead man switch at full power. The train car was accelerating to its full speed of sixty miles an hour, but had only reached about twenty-five. Richards hurled himself through the jammed-open doors, landing on the shoulders of his armored vest, protecting himself from a crippling injury. Tumbling in the gravel, he slowed as the train car accelerated.

The improvised missile came to a sudden halt at the end of the tunnel, crumpling into a mangled mass of metal. Men emplaced on the train platform screamed out in surprise and pain, and Richards smiled.

"Kamikaze, motherfuckers," the death dealer whispered. Weist was by his side, helping him to his feet, stuffing his AK into his hands.

"Fire in the hole!" Weist shouted. He triggered his grenade launcher, spearing a 40 mm shell into the distance. The detonation four hundred yards downrange was a loud pop to Richards's ears, a low throaty bass, as opposed to the shrill screams of agonized enemies. Their cries of pain increased in intensity as Weist's shrapnel rained down on them.

"Light it up!" Weist ordered, and .30-caliber bullets roared in the tunnel. The blunt suppressors on the ends of their AKs controlled the pressure of the autoweapons, muffling their brain-crushing muzzle-blasts in the confines of the tunnel, but with all the weapons going off at once, it was still a cacophony of chugging rifles.

The scope on Richards's rifle brought a Rose Initiative defender into sharp definition, and the rogue crusader triggered his AK. A snarl of 7.62 mm rounds tore into the man's chest, steel-cored ammunition punching hard into his body armor. He jerked, spitting up blood for a moment, then collapsed lifeless.

"Recon," Weist called.

Richards and the two designated scouts of the infiltration team moved forward. It was his mission, and he intended to lead from the front. The trio of commandos advanced down the tunnel, anticipating the gunfire of an Initiative soldier who was playing possum. When they got to the platform, strewn with train wreckage and bloody corpses, Richards gave the call for the main force to move up. The initial thunder and shock of the train crash, followed up by a wave of shrapnel and bullets, had cleared out the defenders. A few bloody trails smeared along the floor, leading to a pair of heavy, armored doors, but Richards had anticipated that.

"Breaching charges," Richards called.

Like a well-oiled machine, the commandos rushed to the doors, planting packets of high explosives into the seams and hinges of the armored gateway. Lines of detonation cord crisscrossed the center of the double doors, a hot-burning, high-velocity version of the cord meant to carve its way through rolled, heavy steel like it was butter. Weist's warriors had finished setting the charges in the space of a minute, and they rushed down into the tunnel, out of the blast radius. Richards triggered the detonation.

The kinetic force released by the exploding cable, coupled with the hammer blow impacts of the pack charges at various stress points, ripped the two-foot steel doors apart, stretching and bending them as if they were clay. Richards and Weist fired their grenade launchers through the new opening, Weist clearing the archway with a buckshot shell, while Richards rebounded a fragmentation grenade off the far wall, skipping it farther down the new tunnel. The delayed detonation was accompanied by shouts of pain, and a severed limb launched out onto the shattered platform.

"Make a hole and make it wide," Weist shouted.

His commandos surged forward, AKs pouring steel-cored rounds into the enemy corridor. The Rose Initiative gunmen who had taken up defensive positions were caught flat-footed, stunned by the powerful concussion of Richards's grenade. Armor-piercing bullets snapped through body armor, punching deeply into vulnerable organs. At the far end of the new tunnel, a machine gun opened up, and two of Weist's warriors were decapitated by the whipsaw stream of heavy bullets. Their armored helmets were crushed and torn by the 7.62 mm NATO rounds spitting out of the M-60 that the defenders had in place. Weist and Richards responded with more grenade launches, but the thunder of the light machine guns continued unabated, despite the eruptions of the 40 mm shells.

Richards glanced over the top and saw what had stopped their grenades.

"They've got chain-link fence hung in front of the M-60s," Richards explained.

"Our grenades can't fit through the links, but that doesn't stop their fire," Weist snarled. "It's the same tactics we use on tanks against RPG fire."

"Buckshot," Richards said. "Small pellets, and no impact fuse."

"Grenadiers! Buck on three!" Weist called to his team.

Richards glanced back down the tunnel and saw a light glimmering in the distance. His jaw tensed as he realized that his pursuer was on his way. The crippling of the other transport car hadn't stopped him. He'd obtained some form of maintenance vehicle from a storage tunnel.

"Three!" Weist shouted. Richards added his buckshot round to the fusillade of a half-dozen 40 mm grenade launchers transformed into giant shotguns. Three thousand .36-caliber balls sliced the air, slipping between chain links and careened across the tops of sandbags, tearing into the pair of M-60 gunners and their loaders. Their bodies were swatted aside as if by the hand of an invisible giant, and Richards led the charge into the tunnel, AK-47 tracking, ready to unleash a stinging blast of heavy caliber rounds. He paused only long enough to inform Weist that his nemesis was on their tail.

Weist stopped and pointed to a fire team. "Stop him. I don't care how."

The quartet of commandos nodded and rushed to take up their defensive positions.

Richards continued on, racing toward his final conflict with Hamilton Thorn for control of the Rose Initiative's Arsenal.

THE EXECUTIONER HEARD the sounds of autofire dissipate from down the tunnel. He was hot on Cameron Richards's trail, and the man had just bypassed another level of Rose Initiative security. Rifle fire plinked against the grille of the old pickup truck, but Bolan hadn't come this far to be stopped by an enemy blockade. He hit the brakes on the truck and got out, using the vehicle as cover. He grabbed a dead commando's AK-47 and looked through its scope to get his bearings on Richards's back-door defense.

Four men, armed with rifles, were firing ranging shots in order to get their bearings on him. At over four hundred yards, they were pressing the limits of the medium-powered .30-caliber COMBLOC rounds in the rifles. Bolan used the crosshatches on the crosshairs of his scope to gauge the amount of bullet drop he had to make up for. He pulled the trigger, targeting one of the commandos, and an instant later, the gunman's shoulder exploded. Bolan adjusted for windage, and fired a second shot, 123-grains of steel-cored copper-jacketed devastation striking the man in the goggles. The protective plastic imploded, unable to withstand the high-momentum, midweight bullet and allowing it to core through the rifleman's eye socket. The deformed slug came to a halt in the commando's brain.

The remaining gunmen opened fire, going full-auto and hoping they could walk their bullets onto target against the Executioner. Bolan maintained his cool, keeping his head low. The headlights of the pickup truck were on, creating a void of blackness that the enemy marksmen couldn't see past. The suppressed muzzle-flash of the AK was invisible compared to the flare of the pickup's lamps.

The second of Weist's soldiers jerked violently, his nose disintegrating under Bolan's shot. The two remaining enemy riflemen scrambled, evacuating their firing positions. Unfortunately for one of the commandos, his tactical movement exposed him to another of the Executioner's deadly precision bullets, and he tumbled lifelessly to the ground.

Bolan tracked the last of the gunmen, then ducked back behind cover as sparks exploded on the metal skin of the pickup truck. He glanced around the fender and saw that the headlights had been taken out. He felt a round glance off the side of the truck and pluck at his biceps. The enemy gunner had either gotten lucky, or his eyes were readjusting to the darkness, enabling him to utilize his scope. The Executioner crawled into the bed of the pickup, using the cab as protection. He'd seen a maintenance spotlight in the back, and he turned it on. The old lamp still had some juice in its battery, and the fat, high-candlepower bulb put out a dazzling burst of light. With the windshield and rear window of the cab knocked out by the enemy squad's fire, the light wasn't diffused.

As blindness set in for his enemy, Bolan dropped over the side of the pickup's bed, charging up the tracks. The distant sniper maintained his focus on the bulk of the stopped vehicle, popping off shots to take out the powerful lamp that had thrown up a fog of illumination. The Executioner was counting on his opponent to repeat a previous successful tactic, and the man obliged him. The rifleman didn't expect Bolan to race on foot into the hot muzzle of an emplaced AK.

Bolan knew his ruse wouldn't last long, but as the pe-

riphery of the lamp's cone of light lit him up, he received
another reprieve. The rifleman took out the spotlight, the
bullet shattering the bulb and tossing the train tunnel back
into dim gloom. It would take a few moments for the
gunner's eyes to adjust to the relative darkness, but by that
time, Bolan had closed to three hundred yards. He threw
himself prone again. While closer, enabling more precision
from his assault rifle, it also meant that the enemy had it
easier trying to gauge his shots.

What Weist's commando didn't share with Bolan,
however, was an intimacy with the Kalashnikov born
through countless conflicts shooting it and being shot at
with it. The Executioner didn't need the scope at that
range, his experience with the weapon system taking
over. The enemy rifleman spun as rifle rounds chopped
into his neck and arm. Bolan tapped off another short
burst, this one catching the wounded gunman through the
center of his throat, the second and third rounds punching
into his Kevlar vest and churning through his rib cage
underneath.

Bolan got to his feet and ran. He knew that the pickup truck
had seen its last miles, and a quick glance back at the smoking
engine confirmed that he wouldn't get the vehicle moving
again. It was three hundred yards to the wrecked train
platform, and then no telling how far into the depths of the
Rose Initiative facility. Once he completed the journey, he had
at least eighteen of Richards's commandos, and no telling
how many of the Initiative's defense forces, left to fight.

Bolan settled into a ground-eating pace, a long-distance
gait that would keep him from ending up breathless at the
end of the run.

CAMERON RICHARDS WATCHED another of his team collapse, a figure eight of autofire slashed into his chest. Richards triggered his AK in response, a stream of bullets obliterating the face of a Rose Initiative defender. The madness of pitched combat raged around him, gunfire streaking through the air so thick, he could see the yellow claw marks that the slugs cut in the air by their super-heated passage. The world around him was a continuous roar of gunfire and grenade detonations as the hallway they'd finally breached was a fortress line.

Machine guns, assault rifles and grenades joined in a ca-cophony of violence and bloodshed as Richards's force and the Initiative each strove to exterminate the other side. It was a battle where no quarter could be given or taken. The only outcome was death for one combatant or the other. Richards was in the process of reloading when a figure leaped on him, brandishing a knife. The AK toppled from his grasp as the death dealer was shoved to the floor. With one hand locked on the knife wrist of the Initiative guard, he wrapped his other hand around the grip of his Taurus Raging Bull, swiv-eling the big .44 Magnum revolver around and triggering it. The massive bullet punched into the knife-man's belly, churning up and under his ribs to split his heart in two. The lethal impact made the man reflexively convulse, and he collapsed on the floor at Richards's side. Another Initiative sentry spotted the latest kill and fired a burst in Richards's direction.

The assassin huddled tightly behind the corpse of the man he'd killed, letting the inert body soak up bullets like a sponge. When the guard stopped in realization that he was pumping his own comrade full of slugs, Richards popped up and hammered out two quick .44 Magnum slugs at the rifleman. The 300-grain skull-smashers turned the wall behind the gunman into a modern art painting composed of blood. Richards dropped his hand to pull his Beretta, since he needed the firepower to get to his rifle. He was completely surrounded by the screams of the dying, and he spotted Weist hold up a dying man as a human shield, moving toward a fallen light machine gun that had been lost in the battle. Weist's .45 cracked, spitting hot lead to cover his retreat to the powerful weapon.

Richards swung his Beretta around and gave Weist some cover fire, punching 9 mm rounds into the backs and heads of Rose Initiative soldiers who were trying to slow the commando leader. One of the defenders whirled as he saw his compatriots jerking under the sudden onslaught of handgun fire and leveled a 12-gauge shotgun at Richards's gut. The Taurus bellowed before the shotgunner could trigger his own cannon, sprawling the hapless guard on the ground, missing half of his face.

Weist ditched his human shield and scooped up the M-60 machine gun from the floor. He triggered the weapon, sweeping the ranks of Initiative defenders with a hail of 7.62 mm NATO rounds. Richards charged, scooping up the fallen shotgun and contributing a storm of 12-gauge thunder to the high-velocity NATO lightning unleashed by Weist. Bodies crumpled under the brutal two-pronged onslaught, the heavy-caliber weaponry wielded by the invading pair overwhelming the guards. When the shotgun locked empty, Richards continued on, firing with his Beretta, but by then, it was simply a cleanup.

Weist surveyed his surviving commandos. There were

eleven left, counting himself and Richards. "Less than half the force we came in with."

"I know," Richards answered, regret painting his words. "They'll be honored in the coming world."

Weist nodded. "Start gathering firepower. We've used up a lot of our ammo taking this point."

Weist loaded another belt into his captured machine gun and grinned, throwing the bolt back to lock a round in place. His grin disappeared in shock as he swung the M-60 toward Richards.

Richards scanned the corpses. They'd encountered a defensive force that had lost forty men so far. The savagery of the combat had seemed so much more intense because of the volume of gunfire, but lateral movement and cover had pushed the conflict to a higher fever pitch.

"Get down, Cam!"

Richards dived for cover, catching movement out of the corner of his eye. Weist opened fire on the intruder.

"Move! I'll hold him off!" Weist shouted.

Cameron Richards, the death dealer gone rogue, took off, leading the ragtag remainder of the invasion force to wrest control of the Rose Initiative's stockpile of doom.

The Executioner's opening salvo on Richards and Weist's remaining soldiers was wasted. The trauma plates inserted into Weist's load-bearing vest stopped even the steel-cored AK ammunition. The commando opened up with the M-60 and Bolan dived to the side, feeling the slicing ravages of machine-gun bullets raking across his leg. One bullet went through the muscle, but fortunately none of the slugs contacted his femur or his femoral artery, otherwise he'd have been in a world of trouble.

Still, the leg was bloody, and walking on it would be a struggle. Bolan let the AK-47 clatter to the floor, going for his OA-93 machine pistol.

Bolan knew that Richards and the remaining members of the commando team were still on the move. What he didn't know was what Richards needed to unleash the weapons stored in the Arsenal. If there was a control room, then the death dealer could possibly activate his superweapons from one spot. Otherwise, the ten or so men available would have to cart their stockpile of mass destruction on foot.

With the wreckage back at the train platform, it was a sure thing that ten men were going to have a difficult time moving the equipment, especially if they went toward the White House grounds, ten miles away.

What mattered at the moment, though, was Weist and

his machine gun. Bolan fired around the corner, the machine pistol spitting death. He attempted to get the front sight on Weist's head, but a round nicked his shoulder, spinning him back behind the corner.

"You fight a warrior for the cause, coward!" Weist bellowed. "You hide, while I stand strong, a symbol of the true American fighting man."

Bolan took a moment to pull a roll of duct tape and some first-aid gauze from his vest. He needed to control the bleeding in his leg and, since Weist didn't seem to be interested in conserving ammunition, he'd let the madman run down his belt. Pressing squares of gauze to his through-and-through gunshot wounds and the creases along his skin, he taped the swatches in place, securing them firmly. The process was quick and messy, his hands stained with blood, but he had staunched the nonarterial bleeding. He'd be good for a while with the duct tape and sterile gauze covering his injuries. He checked his shoulder and saw that his armor was torn, but the bullet had only raised a bruise beneath his blacksuit top.

Bolan unhooked a grenade from his belt and pulled the pin on it.

"I'd like to accommodate your delusions, Weist," Bolan shouted over the din of the M-60.

"What delusion?" Weist growled, holding his fire for a moment.

Bolan tossed the grenade around the corner. "That you're a warrior, and that you're worth my time."

Weist screamed in rage, holding down the trigger on his M-60, but the Executioner was back around the corner. Bullets sparked harmlessly off the wall a moment before the fragmentation grenade detonated. The bent and twisted body of the machine gun skidded in front of Bolan, covered in a smear of blood and guts. He hauled himself to his feet and turned the corner and saw Weist—what was left of him.

Bolan started in the direction Richards and his remaining team had run in when his hands-free radio sparked to life.

"Striker," Grimaldi spoke up. "Splashed the other XH-92 in the Potomac. Survivors in both birds to be rounded up by Hal's people. Need support?"

"I traveled ten miles underground. I have no idea where I am, though," Bolan returned. "Bear?"

"We can barely hear you, Striker," Kurtzman responded. "But we've got your position triangulated. I can send Jack over the area, but there's nothing there."

"This might have been an emergency cold war base. We've got the high-speed train from the White House—" Bolan said.

"We can't get in any way except from the access back at the White House," Carmen Delahunt interrupted.

"That'll be tough. I took the only working vehicle down the train tunnel," Bolan said. "They wrecked both trains and shot up the maintenance truck."

Bolan moved along as fast as he could. His leg throbbed, but he could maneuver fairly well. He scanned the corridor ahead of him, looking for signs of Richards and his strike force, fighting through his injury.

"We could get a team of blacksuits on-site," Kurtzman suggested. "Motorcycles."

"Get what you can over here," Bolan said.

He heard a fresh bout of gunfire in the distance, and broke into a ground-eating jog. There'd be time enough to favor his injured leg when the threat of Cameron Richards was ended.

HAMILTON THORN SNEERED as Richards's commandos writhed under the assault of the remote-controlled robot he had under his command. With his sixty men in the facility, he thought they'd have been more than a match for a mere two dozen commandos, and yet, half of the commandos were still alive. Fortunately, the remote drone, equipped with a pair of M-249 Squad Automatic Weapons, proved a harder nut to crack. With its vulnerable hydraulics and electronic guts protected by inch-thick steel panels, the battle drone had cut down three of the enemy gunmen from its secreted position at a corner. The SAWs ripped off bursts at 800 rounds per minute, and were fed by special 500-round belts designed for the combat robot.

Thorn grinned as he saw a fourth gunman's chest explode. He was watching the assault through the drone's camera. Splashes of blood hit the lens, obstructing Thorn's view, but with the deep reservoirs of the SAW's ammunition supply, and the other optics on the battle drone, the Rose Initiative leader simply rolled his robot around with gleeful abandon, hammering out long bursts.

He laughed out loud as another man's head imploded under the assault of a prolonged burst. He leaned down to the microphone.

"What fun! Who'd have thought an old man could kick all of your sissy asses single-handedly?" Thorn shouted.

"Burn in hell!" Richards bellowed.

Thorn heard the sound of a grenade-launcher firing, and suddenly half of the cameras were knocked out of commission on his control panel. He swiveled the robot, machine-gun fire tracking his former top death dealer. Richards was quick, running faster than the treads of the drone could spin.

A sixth commando folded over Thorn's SAW burst, an unintended kill, but a satisfying one nonetheless he thought.

The grenade launcher fired again, and the rest of the cameras were out of commission. Thorn switched a monitor over to the security cameras secreted in mirrored domes outside the control room. The robot still stood, and it responded to Thorn's controls. Only its eyes seemed to have been knocked off-line, but when Thorn pulled the trigger, only one of the SAWs fired.

That one, however, scored a glancing hit on Richards.

"Ah, good show, Cameron, but the house wins again," Thorn called over his microphone.

A commando rushed up and stuffed a hand grenade into a camera lens hole that had been vacated. That moment of bravado cost the commando his life. The battle drone detonated, a chunk of armor plating slicing the fleeing soldier in two.

Richards grabbed the wall and hauled himself to his feet. Blood soaked his left side, and his arm hung limp.

"The house hasn't won yet, old man!" Richards barked defiantly. He reached into his holster and drew the long barreled Magnum revolver he favored. "Does anyone still have a breaching charge?"

There were two commandos with Richards. One of them produced a packet of high explosives, and Thorn frowned. He glanced to his security monitors and spotted a squad of Rose Initiative gunmen closing in on Richards and the control room. They'd arrive in time to harass the surviving commandos.

"You won't have time to place that," Thorn growled. "Your doom is coming."

Richards, his face bloody and haggard, looked up at the mirrored dome. He could see the enemy strike force massing around the corner, ready to burst into the open to take him down.

"Damn you, Thorn! Damn you!" Richards shouted.

"Gentlemen, remove this rubbish from my doorstep!" Thorn shouted.

Hamilton Thorn closed his eyes, waiting for the chatter of autofire to signal the end of his pest problem.

CAMERON RICHARDS HEARD an automatic weapon cut loose from around the corner, and he charged forward, the big .44 Magnum Taurus locked in his fist. Rose Initiative fighters lurched into the hallway, and Richards punched a hole in one of the gunmen, ending his life with a dramatic spray of gore issuing from his skull. However, the man fell all wrong, and Richards realized that the enemy gunmen were being fired upon from behind. His fellow commandos threw in on the flanking attack on the suddenly surprised Initiative team, two forces cutting the gunners down in a cross fire.

Richards dropped the empty Taurus, then fished out his Beretta.

A tall, grim figure in combat black, one leg swathed in duct tape, limp out into the open. Cold blue eyes regarded Richards and his men.

"No!" came a bellow over the loudspeakers.

"Richards," the Executioner said.

"Who are you," Richards asked. "Got a name?"

Bolan dumped the empty magazine from his machine pistol, fitting another into place. He walked closer to the trio, his weapon pointed at the floor. He looked at the half-fastened breaching charge on the door. "So, the head shed of the Rose Initiative's behind those doors?"

"You're calling a truce?" Richards asked.

"A temporary one," Bolan answered. "The way I see it, the Initiative is a far bigger threat than you are."

Richards wiped his wrist across his forehead and nodded. "Yeah. I guess I could use the help against Thorn."

Bolan helped to fasten and set the breaching charge, while Richards and the others reloaded their weapons.

"The man doesn't have a bolt-hole like Cornell did, does he?" Bolan asked.

Richards shrugged. "You've got me. All I know is, he had a combat drone out there that wiped out most of the remainder of my men."

Bolan nodded. Richards thumbed the firing button on the detonator, and the breaching charge tore the doors off Thorn's control room. Instantly, gunfire erupted from within, catching one of the last two commandos flat-footed. Bullets tore into the hapless mercenary, but Richards fired his Beretta hard and fast. The extended 20-round magazine in his pistol ran dry, but the death dealer knew that he had taken out two of Thorn's last line of defense. He stuffed the Beretta into his web belt, dumped the magazine and slapped a fresh one home, all one-handed. Pulling the pistol free, he thumbed the slide-lock lever and chambered a round.

Bolan and the last remaining commando hosed the control room with their autoweapons, taking down more of Thorn's bodyguards. The last line of defense was a hard one, though, and a shotgun blast tore the head off the last of Weist's warriors. The Executioner transitioned from his empty machine pistol to his Desert Eagle, pumping .44 Magnum rounds into the shotgunner.

"Damn it!" Thorn shouted.

"Lose something?" Richards called out.

An assault rifle chattered, driving the injured assassin back behind cover. Bolan fired rounds in the direction of the muzzle-flash, but a stream of bullets drove him out of the fight, too. He looked across to Richards, who set down his Beretta and reached to his belt for a grenade.

"I think he's upset," Richards quipped.

Bolan plucked a grenade of his own from his harness. "On three?"

Richards nodded.

Bolan pulled the pin from his grenade. "After he's done, it's over."

"I know," Richards responded.

The pair lobbed their grenades and ducked behind cover. The two minibombs detonated in unison, their shock waves rocking the control room. They paused for a moment, then heard the chatter of the assault rifle again, bullets searing through the shattered doorway.

"We didn't get him," Richards said.

"Control panels probably shielded him," Bolan said. "Any more grenades?"

"Used them all up," Richards responded. He rested his head against the wall. "Why didn't you finish the job when you had the drop on us?"

"My machine pistol was empty," Bolan admitted. "Why didn't you shoot?"

"I was curious about you," Richards stated. "All the years of stalking around the covert operations arena, I'd heard about someone like you."

"Disappointed?" Bolan asked.

Richards grinned. "Shame we never worked together."

"No, it's not," Bolan said.

Richards nodded. "In a different world, maybe."

"Maybe," Bolan repeated. "At least you're not justifying your ways to me like Spelling."

"Where's Winslow?" Richards asked.

"On his way to prison," Bolan told him.

"Winslow won't last long in jail. He'll find a way to kill himself," Richards responded. "As for my justification? I ate the shit the world gave me, and was too fucking stupid to look for the right path out of my hole. I could blame my dad, or that bastard in there, but it was me. I found the path of least resistance, and it was straight to damnation."

Bolan rummaged through the gear belts of the dead commandos Richards had brought with him. He found several stun-shock grenades and rolled a couple of them to Richards.

"No speech?" Richards asked.

"You said what had to be said. You've seen what you've done wrong," Bolan replied. "No more need for reproach."

Richards hooked his thumb through the ring on the pin of the stun grenade. "He was protected from shrapnel. But I doubt he's ready for this."

"It'll at least buy us a few more seconds," Bolan said, popping the pins on two of his grenades. He had two more stuffed in his web belt, ready to go.

"Any word on my pilot?" Richards asked.

"Fished out of the Potomac," Bolan said.

"He never pulled the trigger on anyone," Richards said. "Go easy on him."

Bolan tilted his head, then nodded. "On three."

The pair launched their stun grenades, and Bolan rapidly pulled and threw his backup pair. The five distraction devices thundered in the confines of Thorn's control room, shock waves and searing flashes spearing painfully through the last bastion of the Rose Initiative. Bolan and Richards got up and entered, their Magnums tracking.

Thorn was sprawled on the floor, bleeding from the head where a shock-grenade detonator had split the skin as it bounced off his skull. The stunned conspirator crawled toward his fallen assault rifle, but neither the Executioner, nor his death dealing temporary ally were in the mood for fairness. They were both too badly hurt and exhausted after a week of arduous struggle. They emptied their handguns into Thorn's body, massive bullets excavating horrific tunnels through his vital organs.

Richards let his .44 drop to the ground, then pulled his Beretta and put one last shot into Thorn's ruptured skull. "That's for stealing my ideals, you bastard."

Bolan looked at the sad, bloody figure before him.

"Even if I beat you to the draw, I'm crippled, losing too much blood and alone. There's no way I could do anything with the Initiative's arsenal," Richards said.

"I know," Bolan answered.

"I thought maybe I could herald in a better world," Richards told Bolan. He looked at the pulped remnants of the Rose Initiative leadership and sighed. "Is there such a thing?"

"Millions of people are working toward it, one day at a time. Change doesn't come through blood and thunder. I just use it to buy time for the real heroes to get their work completed," Bolan explained. "My guns are for those who disrupt the process of healing and betterment."

Richards looked up and smiled. He swallowed to choke

back a sob. "And that's our real difference there. You believe in redemption and the human spirit."

Bolan nodded grimly, and his eyes dropped to the Beretta in his opponent's fist. His own 93-R was nestled in its shoulder holster. It would go into action much slower than a handgun already in the death dealer's hand.

Richards's Beretta rose swiftly. Bolan let his injured leg fold beneath him, pulling him out of the path of fire as he reached for his own 9 mm. When Bolan struck the ground, a spear of pain rose from his shot-up thigh, but his grip was firm on the 93-R. The machine pistol snapped out of its holster, the long barrel whipping toward Richards who was diving for cover himself.

A pull of the trigger, and the Executioner sent a salvo of 9 mm rounds into Richards, catching him in the stomach, rather than his head. The man's body armor held, just as Bolan's did when Richards finally brought his own Beretta onto target. Bolan grunted under the impacts against his Kevlar vest and fired off another triburst of 9 mm judgments

Richards ducked his head, his hair flying as a single bullet skimmed his scalp. Bolan winced as a round struck the frame of his Beretta, tearing the weapon from his grasp. The Executioner rolled, throwing himself behind cover as the death dealer lurched into the open, tracking him.

Richards had a death grip on his Beretta, and it was the only thing that saved his life when Bolan burst from behind a grenade-savaged counter, wrapping both hands around Richards's forearm. The renegade assassin swung to greet the soldier, forehead impacting against Bolan's nose. Dazed, the Executioner staggered away from Richards, but not before tearing the pistol out of his grasp.

Richards went for a knife on his harness, drawing the steel blade in a lightning movement. The tip whistled through the air, but Bolan turned into the swing, catching the cutting edge against his vest. Magazines for his machine pistol provided enough reinforcement to the Kevlar vest to stop the knife from sinking into his rib cage.

Richards bit down hard on the Executioner's neck, incisors splitting skin. Bolan's shoulders had shrugged reflexively at the last moment, the teeth stabbing into muscle, rather than an exposed jugular.

With a twist, Bolan hurled Richards to the floor and punched down hard.

Cameron Richards's larynx shattered, his windpipe collapsing as the Executioner's lethal knuckle strike landed. Richards's eyes bugged out, and he dropped the knife, reaching for his crushed throat as blood poured over his lips.

In an instant, the renegade assassin was dead, having paid for his crimes.

Bolan staggered to his feet, then went to look for the Arsenal.

Epilogue

Hal Brognola was at the train platform on the White House side of the tunnel when the Executioner rolled the battered, shot-up pickup truck to a halt. The big Fed looked at Bolan, his face aghast at the blood spattered all over the warrior as he got out of the truck. Brognola noted a flap of skin torn on his neck, a human bite wound.

"What happened?" Brognola asked.

Bolan staggered up the steps, helped along by a group of blacksuits "I finished the job."

Brognola nodded, looking down the tunnel. "We're going to send a team down."

"Don't," Bolan said. He reached into his pocket and pulled out a detonator. "Just push the button."

"But what about the stockpile of weaponry?" Brognola asked.

The Executioner glanced back down the tracks. "Hal, I know you trust our government. The thing is, the very existence of the Rose Initiative proves that no good intentions last forever. The agency was constructed to defend this nation, to provide it with a covert line of defense. But over time, the power he accumulated corrupted its leader."

Brognola looked at the detonator in Bolan's hand. "But the advantages we could have… From what I've seen of Spelling's reports…"

"No, Hal," Bolan said. "I looked through the Arsenal. There are things there that have no right existing in this world. To have them under the control of any man is wrong."

Brognola frowned.

"What happened to Spelling?" Bolan asked.

"He got hold of something and hung himself in his cell," Brognola answered.

Bolan sighed. "And he was looking for his own second chance."

"He played you against his cousin, Striker," Brognola replied. "He wanted all of this bloodshed to happen."

Bolan nodded, then handed over the detonator.

Brognola held the little red button, feeling its insignificant weight in his beefy paw.

"Administrations might be trusted, even if they do make mistakes," Bolan continued. "But what about renegades like Thorn, or Spelling?"

Brognola did a double take when he realized that the Executioner hadn't mentioned Cameron Richards. "Where is Richards?"

"Dead," Bolan said. "He accepted his judgment, but not without a fight."

Brognola hefted the detonator. "And this will take out... what?"

"Contagion samples. Poisons. Electronic warfare weaponry of insidious design," Bolan explained. "Things that could render large tracts of the planet inhospitable."

"No nukes?" Brognola asked.

"More than a few, but they're buried deeply," Bolan replied. "The vault goes down into the bedrock."

Brognola nodded, then mashed his thumb against the detonator. The ground beneath them shook violently.

"That would be the nuke I set up to clean out the stock-pile," Bolan stated. "Twenty kilotons."

"The guys monitoring seismic activity will freak over this, then," Brognola said. "We're not in danger here, are we?"

Bolan shook his head. "Too much concrete and bedrock between the bomb and the surface."

Brognola looked at the radio detonator and gave a low whistle. "You're right. Power does corrupt. I never set off a nuclear warhead by myself before."

Bolan shrugged. "Enough of a rush to make it a habit, old friend?"

Brognola dropped the detonator onto the platform and crushed it beneath his heel. "Let's just keep the detonators attached to the big bombs out of my hands for a long time."

Bolan smiled weakly.

"Let's get you home, Striker. You need some R and R."

Bolan let out a relaxed breath. "That's the first sugges-tion in a long time I don't have an issue with."

Bolan, helped by his friend Brognola, worked his way up the steps. By the time he was buckled into *Dragon-slayer*'s cabin, the Executioner slept the sleep of the righ-teous, untroubled and serene.

Don Pendleton's Mack Bolan®

Hard Passage

A Russian-Jihadist alliance arms America's street gangs with killer firepower...

Acting as unofficial backup to a CIA mission in St. Petersburg, Russia, Mack Bolan learns of a deal brokered between militant Russian youth gangs and Jihadists—aimed at the United States. Bolan aims to shake up the enemy's infrastructure, derail its timetable and declare total war. But the fuse is lit... and America's most violent gangs are being armed and primed to unleash the enemy's ultimate shocking agenda....

Available March 2009 wherever books are sold.

TAKE 'EM FREE

2 action-packed novels plus a mystery bonus

NO RISK
NO OBLIGATION TO BUY

ROOM 59

CLIFF RYDER

BLACK WIDOW

An isolated international incident turns into mass murder....

Young women widowed in Chechnya's bloody conflict with Russia are now willing suicide bombers. Room 59 wants an agent to go undercover as one of the Black Widows—and they recruit MI-6 operative Ajza Manaev. In a world where loyalties and the playing field are often shifting, Ajza is inducted by hellfire into Room 59's hard and fast rule. She's on her own.

Available April 2009
wherever books are sold.

GOLD EAGLE ®